mary-kate olsen   as

GETTING
THERE

*Sweet 16
and
Licensed
to Drive*

GETTING THERE

By Eliza Willard

Selected scenes based on the teleplay

by Michael Swerdlick

HarperEntertainment

An Imprint of HarperCollins*Publishers*

A PARACHUTE PRESS BOOK

A PARACHUTE PRESS BOOK

Parachute Publishing, L.L.C.
156 Fifth Avenue, Suite 302
New York, NY 10010

Published by
■HarperEntertainment
An Imprint of HarperCollins*Publishers*
10 East 53rd Street, New York, NY 10022-5299

SWEET 16 books are created and produced by Parachute Press, L.L.C., in cooperation with Dualstar Publications, a division of Dualstar Entertainment Group, LLC., published by HarperEntertainment, an imprint of HarperCollins Publishers.

ISBN 0-06-051595-3

HarperCollins®, ■®, and HarperEntertainment™ are trademarks of HarperCollins Publishers Inc.

First printing: July 2002

Printed in the United States of America

Visit HarperEntertainment on the World Wide Web at
www.harpercollins.com

10 9 8 7 6 5 4 3 2

prologue

"**A**ll right!" Kylie Hunter called out. "Licensed to drive!" The wind whipped through her blond hair as she zoomed down the highway in her brand-new pink Ford Mustang convertible.

"The sun shining on our faces, the wind in our hair, the open road!" Kylie exclaimed. "Isn't this great."

"Enough with the infomercial, Kylie," Taylor Hunter grumbled. Kylie and Taylor were sixteen-year-old twin sisters. "When do I drive?"

"You will," Kylie told her.

Taylor slouched in her seat. Kylie always hogged the car. She and Taylor had turned sixteen six months earlier. Their parents had given them the convertible as a birthday present. Having a car changed their lives, totally for the better. Now Kylie and Taylor were mobile! They were free!

Their friends Jenn and Lyndi, both seventeen, sat in the backseat of the car.

"Henry Ford is the coolest," Jenn said, patting the Mustang.

"Henry Ford?" Lyndi asked. "He's a junior, right?"

Taylor turned around in her seat. "Henry Ford started the Ford Motor Company," she informed Lyndi. "Horseless carriages? Does American history ring a bell? Last fall?"

"Oh, yeah." Lyndi pressed her curly, light brown hair to her head. The wind was making it frizz. "Henry Ford was the president, right?"

"That was Gerald Ford," Kylie corrected Lyndi. Lyndi could be such an airhead sometimes.

"There are too many Fords," Lyndi complained. "Do you think Mr. Ford would mind if we put the top up? It's messing my hair."

"No way," Kylie said. "Top down rocks."

Taylor studied her map. "From here we take I-15. Then it's only six hundred miles to Salt Lake City and the Winter Olympics. Our first road trip!"

Taylor high-fived Kylie. Lyndi crouched down in her seat. "Five hundred and forty-four miles?" She groaned. "That's a lot of wind. . . ."

Taylor's cell phone rang. She checked the caller ID. "It's the guys," she told the others. "Hey, Sam," she said into the phone.

The girls' friends Sam, Danny, and Toast were cruising to Salt Lake City in a vintage 1970 Cadillac that belonged to Toast's dad. The plan was to meet the girls in Utah for a week of snowboarding, skiing, and Olympics watching.

"What are you all up to?" Sam asked Taylor.

"Well, Lyndi is proving that she needs to retake U.S. history," Taylor reported.

"We're going to stop for something to eat," Sam said.

Taylor eyed her watch. "Didn't you just eat forty minutes ago?"

"We have Toast with us, remember?" Sam said.

Taylor laughed. Toast was cute, but he ate constantly. He never got full. And he was kind of a mess.

"Want to join us?" Sam asked.

"No, thanks," Taylor replied. "This journey began six months ago when we got our car and started planning our trip to the Olympics. We're not stopping now."

I pressed Pause on the remote control. The video image froze in place on the TV screen.

"What do you think so far?" Ashley asked.

"I love it!" Lauren gushed. "It's so cool to see you guys in a movie!"

Ashley and I were sitting with our friends, Lauren and Brittany, on the couch in our basement. A video copy of *Getting There* had arrived that morning. Ashley called Brittany and Lauren right away and invited them over to watch it.

"You guys are on a roll this year," Brittany said. "First you had your Sweet Sixteen party, then you went to MusicFest, and then shooting a movie . . ."

"I have to admit, the last few months have been incredible," I agreed. Last June, Mom and Dad threw us a perfect Sweet Sixteen party, in a gorgeous house overlooking the ocean. Then they gave us a vintage Mustang convertible. And on top of that, Dad arranged for us to work at the coolest rock festival, MusicFest, for the summer.

Then, just as MusicFest was ending, a movie director spotted us and cast us in a movie called *Getting There*!

"What's with that girl Lyndi?" Brittany asked. "Was she really that dim?"

"Actually, she was a brainiac," I told her. "I mean, Delia, the girl who played her, was."

"The guys are hot!" Lauren exclaimed. "Who's the one with the curly blond hair? Sam? He's gorgeous!"

Ashley glanced at me. "I know," she said. "I thought so, too—at first."

"Do any of the characters get together?" Brittany asked. She grinned slyly at us.

"You'll have to watch and find out," I said. "The movie has a great story—but that's nothing compared to what went on behind the scenes. . . ."

chapter one

"Great rehearsal, kids." Don Maneri, the director of *Getting There*, clapped his hands. "Take a lunch break and we'll meet back here at two."

"Hey, Ashley—you're really good," Buddy Jones said to me. "You're, like, a natural actress." He grabbed a muffin from the food table and chomped down on it.

"Thanks," I said. "You're good, too. Definitely 'natural.'"

Buddy was playing Toast in the movie. He looked the part, that was for sure. Buddy was tall and skinny, with large brown puppy-dog eyes and light brown hair. He wasn't too bad-looking, I thought—just kind of rumpled. Slouchy. His hair stuck out in all directions, as if he'd just woken up from a nap. And just like Toast Buddy ate all the time. His stomach was like a bottomless pit.

"Do you want to have lunch together?" Buddy asked me.

"Umm . . ." I started to answer, but Noah Atkins caught my eye as he left the room. My heart did a little flip. Noah played Sam in the movie, and he was totally gorgeous. He was tan from surfing all summer and his curly blond hair shimmered with highlights from the sun.

Mary-Kate is so lucky, I thought. She was playing Kylie Hunter, and I was cast as Taylor. In the movie, Sam has a wicked crush on Kylie. There's even a kissing scene! That meant Mary-Kate would get to kiss Noah.

I glanced at Mary-Kate. She was standing by the door talking to Delia Bishop, who played Lyndi.

"Hey, Ashley—are you okay?" Buddy drew my attention back to him. "Feel like having lunch with me?"

"Oh. Sorry, Buddy," I said. "Thanks, but my sister and I are grabbing sandwiches and going back to our room. We haven't unpacked or anything yet."

"That's cool." Buddy smiled at me. "See you in a couple of hours."

It was our first day on the set of the movie *Getting There.* Mary-Kate and I had dumped our stuff in our motel room early that morning. Then we hurried to a rehearsal, where we met the cast and crew for the first time.

Mary-Kate caught up with me as I headed for

the Orangeview Motel. "Did you know Delia's going to CalTech in the fall?" she asked. "She wants to be a biochemist."

"That's funny." I unlocked the door to our room. "I never would have guessed she was such a brain. She does that spaced-out Lyndi thing so well."

Mary-Kate laughed. "That's why they call it 'acting.'"

We walked into our room and opened our suitcases. Though we were close to home, the entire cast and crew were staying at the Orangeview while we shot the California scenes. Later we were going to Las Vegas and Park City, Utah, to work on location.

Mary-Kate dumped the contents of her suitcase onto her bed. "How fabulous is this?" she said. "I mean, making this movie and everything. I can't believe how lucky we are to be here. And we're perfect for these parts! A movie about two sisters who turn sweet sixteen? It's just so excellent!"

"I know," I agreed. "*And* we get to go to Las Vegas!"

"And Park City!" Mary-Kate added. "It's like going on vacation—only it's part of our job!"

I grinned and high-fived her. "This totally rocks."

"So what do you think so far?" she asked me. "How do you like everybody?"

"They all seem pretty nice." I transferred a pile

of neatly folded tops from my suitcase to a dresser drawer. "What do you think of Noah Atkins?"

"The guy who plays Sam?" Mary-Kate asked. "He's okay."

"Okay?" I sat on the bed and stared at her. "Did you see that smile? Because if you saw him smile and you think he's just okay, there's something wrong with you."

Mary-Kate laughed. "Okay, so he's totally cute. The next Brad Pitt. The trouble is, he knows it. And, anyway, I've got another guy on my mind."

"Jake," I said, thinking of her boyfriend, Jake Impenna. She'd hardly seen him all summer, and I knew she really missed him. "When is he getting here?"

"This afternoon," Mary-Kate replied. "I can't wait! He's bringing his cousin Christina with him. She's moving here from New York."

I pulled a dress out of my suitcase and hung it in the closet. "I never heard him mention a cousin before."

"He hasn't seen her in a few years," Mary-Kate told me. "But she's his favorite cousin. She's staying with his family while her mom gets settled. He was really excited when he told me about it. He says she's a lot of fun."

I lined my shoes up at the bottom of my closet. "I'm done," I said. I unwrapped the sandwich I'd grabbed from a food table on the set. I took a bite and dropped it on my nightstand. "Tuna. Yuck. Want to go downstairs and see what they have at the coffee shop?"

Mary-Kate was sorting through the pile of clothes on her bed, trying to organize it. "No, thanks," she said. "I've got a lot to do here. And, anyway, I like tuna."

"Okay. See you later." I left the room and hurried downstairs to the restaurant attached to the Orangeview.

Some of the cast and crew were scattered throughout the restaurant in small groups. I spotted Noah sitting with Rachel Widmer, who played Jenn, and Kip Cusack, who played Danny. There was an empty seat at their table.

"Mind if I sit here?" I asked, touching the empty chair.

Noah flashed me his gorgeous smile and lightly kicked the chair away from the table. "It's got your name on it," he said. "What's your name again, anyway?"

"Ashley," I told him, sitting down.

"I knew that," Noah said. "I was just testing you."

I laughed. "So what's good here?"

"The burger rocks," Kip said. He was lean and athletic, with medium-length brown hair.

"Everything's kind of greasy." Rachel sniffed,

stirring her iced tea with a long, pink straw.

"You can't go wrong with a turkey sandwich." Noah offered me the uneaten half of his sandwich. "Want a bite?"

"I'll trust you," I replied and ordered a turkey on whole wheat.

"I was just telling the guys about this juice commercial I did last year," Rachel said. "They made me wear a grape costume and painted my face purple. I said, 'Did I spend the last three years studying with Stella Martin for this?'"

She started laughing, a stiff, high-pitched *ha-ha-ha*. I glanced at Noah and Kip. What was she talking about? Noah shrugged.

Rachel must have noticed the blank looks on our faces. "Oh, come on," she said. "Haven't you heard of Stella Martin? The greatest acting coach in Hollywood?"

"Sorry, Rache," Kip said. "Doesn't ring a bell."

Rachel frowned. "Anyway, nobody at school recognized me with all that purple paint on my face—ha-ha-ha! Commercials are great for the money, but they can be so embarrassing! Don't you think, Ashley?"

"I wouldn't know," I replied. "I've never done a commercial."

"You haven't?" Rachel said. "Well, Noah has. Haven't you, Noah?"

Noah ran a hand through his hair. "I don't bother with commercials," he said. "I'd rather be a movie star."

"Well, duh," Rachel shot back. "Everybody would rather be a movie star. But it's not that easy. You have to take what you can get."

Noah's eyes sparkled. *He really could be a movie star,* I thought. *He's so . . . dazzling.*

"We'll see what happens," Noah said.

The waitress set my turkey sandwich on the table. Rachel finished her iced tea. "I've got to go over my lines," she said, standing up. She was tall and pretty with long, thick brown hair. "Kip, want to come rehearse with me?"

Kip slumped in his chair. "Not really."

"Go on, Kip," Noah urged. "You're finished with your burger. I'll keep Ashley company while she eats her sandwich."

Hmm, I thought. *Is he trying to get rid of Kip so he can be alone with me?*

"All right," Kip agreed. He unfolded his body from his chair. "But I'm not going to rehearse. I need a nap. Later."

He followed Rachel out of the coffee shop. Noah pushed his plate away and watched me eat my sandwich.

"It's really great the way you do that," he said.

"Do what?" I asked.

11

"Eat. Chew. Swallow." Noah beamed at me.

I swallowed and put my sandwich down. What was he doing? It was hard to eat with someone watching me so intensely.

"Even the way you set your sandwich on the plate," he added. "Gracefully. Like a queen."

I stared at him. Was he serious?

He gazed into my eyes. I stared back. His eyes were so blue . . . I couldn't tear myself away. It was as if he'd caught me in a tractor beam and I couldn't break free.

"What do you think we are?" he whispered.

"What do you mean?" I asked.

"Like, how would you classify us?"

"Classify?" I was getting confused. What was he talking about? His tractor-beam gaze began to lose its grip on me.

"You know," Noah prompted. "Like, are we a couple?"

A couple? Wait a minute. I thought he was gorgeous, but hadn't he skipped a few steps here?

"Well, maybe we could be a couple someday," I began. "But shouldn't we go on a date or something first?"

Noah frowned and sat up straight. "What's the matter with you, Ashley?" he demanded. "You're doing this all wrong!"

chapter two

"What are you talking about?" I asked. "I don't understand."

"You're not supposed to say anything about going on a date," Noah explained. "You're supposed to say 'We're friends. Friends is good.'"

The lines sounded faintly familiar. But I still had no idea what he was talking about.

"Friends *is* good," I said. "I have no problem with that. But why were you talking about us being a couple?"

Noah laughed. "Not *us*. Sam and Kylie. Don't you know your lines yet?"

Oh. I finally got it. He was rehearsing a scene from the movie! But *he* was the one who had made a mistake. I laughed. "I'm not playing Kylie," I told him. "I'm playing Taylor."

He dropped his head in his hands. "Of course." He moaned. "How could I be so stupid? Your sister,

Mary-Kate, is playing Kylie. I knew that." He lifted his head and gave me that watery-blue gaze again. "I really did know that—I swear. I guess I was just wishing it could be you."

Wow, I thought, getting caught up in his gaze again. The guy is really smooth. Either that—or he really does like me!

"Mary-Kate, this is so cool," Ashley said. A makeup artist brushed her face with powder.

"*So* cool," I agreed. I sat in the chair beside her while Tom, the hairdresser, styled my hair. "Going to wardrobe, getting our makeup done . . . I can't believe this is a job!"

"And in a little while we'll be out on the set, starring in a movie!" Ashley added.

"You're done." Tom whipped the plastic smock off me. "Now get out there and knock 'em dead."

I hopped down from the chair. "Thanks, Tom." I smiled at him.

"You're finished, too," the makeup artist told Ashley. "Ready for your close-up."

Ashley and I left hair and makeup and stepped onto the set. The crew was running around like crazy, setting up the first shot. We sat down in a couple of folding chairs lined up against a wall.

"Hey, girls." Noah sat down next to Ashley. "You're looking hot."

"Thanks," Ashley said.

He waved his script, his lines highlighted in blue. "When I auditioned for this movie, I didn't think they'd give me such a big part!" he said. "I've got a lot of lines to learn."

"Yeah," Ashley agreed. "Us, too."

"It's almost like being in school," Noah said. "Usually, on a nice day like today, I'd hit the surf on my board. I spent the whole summer at the beach." He shook his head a little, so the golden highlights in his hair shimmered.

Oh, brother, I thought. *Is this guy into himself or what?*

"But I guess I can give that up for a few weeks to star in a movie," Noah added. He closed his eyes and grinned.

Ugh, I thought. *He looks so pleased with himself.*

"We had an amazing summer," Ashley told him.

"Really?" Noah asked. "What happened?"

"Well, we turned sixteen in June," Ashley explained, her eyes shining. "Our parents threw us a beautiful party, and they gave us a car. Then we got jobs working at MusicFest—that was wild! Mary-Kate was practically dating a rock star—"

"Don!" Noah interrupted. The director had just walked onto the set, and Noah called out to him. "Don! Can I talk to you a sec?" He jumped up, script in hand, and ran after the director.

Ashley and I stared after him. I couldn't believe the way Noah had just interrupted her!

"That was rude," I commented.

"I'm sure he had to talk to Don about something important," Ashley said.

"Oh, please." I frowned.

"Ashley?" A cameraman approached us. "Will you come with me? I need to check the lighting for your first scene."

"Sure." Ashley followed him onto the set. I watched as he held a light meter up to her face.

"Mary-Kate!" someone called. I turned toward the door of the soundstage. There he was—Jake! I leaped up, ran over, and threw my arms around him.

"Hey," Jake murmured, kissing me. "It's so great to see you!"

"You, too." I hugged him tightly. I'd hardly seen him all summer. I pulled away and looked at him. He was cuter than ever.

"This is my cousin Christina." Jake gestured toward the pale girl standing beside him. She had smooth auburn hair and pretty, delicate features. She was wearing a peasant blouse and low-slung jeans with a wide metal-studded belt. "Christina Lawson, this is Mary-Kate."

She smiled at me. "Jake has been talking about you ever since I got to L.A.," she confided. "He's really missed you."

"Don't tell her that!" Jake playfully slapped her arm. "She's supposed to think I'm too cool to miss her."

"Too late," I joked. "I already know how uncool you are."

He put his arm around my waist and pulled me close. It felt so good to be near him again.

"So this is where you're shooting the movie?" he asked, looking around the big warehouse we were using as a soundstage.

"Yeah," I replied. "Until next week, when we're going to Las Vegas! And Park City after that."

"You're so lucky!" Christina sighed. "It must be exciting to be in this movie!"

"Well, I'll find out soon," I told her. "Today is our first day of shooting."

"You're going to be great," Jake said. "First you're hanging out with rock stars, then you're a movie star. How am I going to keep up with you?"

"Well, you've got basketball camp coming up," I told him. "That's exciting."

He laughed. "Yeah. Basketball camp. It's very glamorous—if you like wind sprints."

"What about me?" Christina put in. "While Jake's away at camp, I'll be sitting at home with my aunt and uncle and eight-year-old and five-year-old cousins. Even basketball camp beats that." She sighed. "I'll be bored out of my mind."

"Why don't you hang out here with me on the set?" I offered. "I mean, if you feel like getting out of the house for a while—"

"Are you kidding?" Christina replied. "That would be excellent! I'd love to!"

"That's a great idea, Mary-Kate," Jake added. "And this way the two of you can get to know each other. My favorite cousin and my girlfriend. You guys are going to be best friends," he predicted.

Jake squeezed my hand. He seemed so happy that Christina and I were getting along.

"Hey, is that your costume for the next scene?" Christina asked me.

I glanced down at the flowered dress that Amy Burke, the wardrobe designer, had given me to wear. "Yeah." I sighed. "It's not exactly my style. I like the other girls' costumes better."

Christina surveyed the other girls as they gathered near the set. "You're right," she agreed. "Maybe this will help." She took off her metal-studded belt and wrapped it around my hips. Then she stepped back to check out the effect. "Much better," she declared.

I hurried to a mirror near the wardrobe room. The belt transformed the dress from "grandma" to "groovy."

"Christina—this is so nice of you!" I cried. "Thank you!"

18

"No problem," she said. Then she giggled. "Hey—my belt is going to be in a movie. It'll be famous!"

"Mary-Kate!" Don, the director, shouted. "We need you over here!"

"Can we stay and watch?" Jake asked.

"Sure," I said. "But try not to laugh at me. Remember—it's my first day!"

I hurried to the set. "Places!" the director called. "And . . . action!"

"Our first road trip!" Kylie exclaimed. She opened the trunk of the Mustang convertible and dropped her backpack inside. Taylor, Jenn, and Lyndi loaded their packs into the trunk. The girls were getting ready for their trip to the Winter Olympics in Park City, Utah. They had started planning the trip six months ago, and now the time to leave had finally arrived. Mr. Hunter recorded the event with a video camera.

"Well," Mrs. Hunter said. "You've been good drivers for six months. I guess you're ready now."

"I still think we should fly to Salt Lake City," Taylor protested.

"Taylor, I know it's hard for you, but relax," Kylie said. "Half the fun is getting there."

"No," Taylor insisted. "The fun is there. Ice hockey, bobsledding, downhill skiing . . ."

"Not to mention your favorite skier, Alex

Reisher," Lyndi added. "Who is totally gorgeous."

"I respect Alex Reisher because he's a brilliantly fast and powerful downhill skier," Taylor declared.

Kylie flashed her a look.

Taylor crumbled under the pressure. "And he's gorgeous," she admitted.

"I second that," Jenn agreed.

"Sure, the Olympics will be fun," Kylie said. "But this trip is about us hanging with our friends, cruising in our car with the wind whipping through our hair. . . ."

Lyndi grabbed the top of her curly head. "My hair . . ." She moaned.

Taylor didn't care about any of that. She just wanted to get there. "Flying takes two hours," she said. "Wind whipping through our hair—eleven hours. I still say flying makes more sense."

"And you are staying in the most amazing ski lodge," Mrs. Hunter reminded them.

"Fireplaces in every bedroom, heated sidewalks, and the best ski instructors anywhere," Mr. Hunter added.

"Thanks, Mom and Dad," Kylie said as she and Taylor hugged their parents.

"I have three favors to ask of you girls," Mr. Hunter said. "One—be smart. Two—be safe."

"And three?" Kylie asked.

"Listen to Mike and Alison," Mr. Hunter said.

"Mike and who-a-son?" Lyndi asked.

"My parents' friends are staying right next door to our rooms," Taylor explained.

Lyndi's face fell. "Oh. Chaperons."

"You are going with young men," Mrs. Hunter reminded us.

"Young, yes," Taylor said. "But men? That's a stretch."

"Speak of the devil," Lyndi said. "Here comes the Toastmobile."

Toast's 1970 Cadillac rumbled up the street, horn honking. Toast was driving, with Danny sitting shotgun and Sam in the backseat. Toast turned toward the driveway but missed it by a few feet, bumping to a stop halfway on the lawn.

"Sorry, Mr. Hunter," Toast called through the car window. He chomped on a doughnut. Taylor spotted the open doughnut box on the seat beside Toast. He'd worked his way through half a dozen already.

"Let's go, girls," Toast said. "Last one to the In-n-Out Burger in Barstow buys lunch!"

"Hold it." Mr. Hunter stopped taping for a minute. "You're not racing."

Danny put on his best please-the-parents face. "Racing? No, sir! That was just a figure of speech. You know, like 'Let's book, we want to bust some phat air.'"

Mr. Hunter frowned.

"Don't worry, Mr. Hunter," Sam added. "We'll be cool. Right, Ky-Ky?"

Kylie looked uncomfortable. "Um—right, Sam-Sam."

Taylor rolled her eyes. "Puh-leeze." Sam had a huge crush on Kylie, and he couldn't be more obvious about it. But Taylor knew that he hadn't won over Kylie yet.

"See you in Barstow, girls," Toast said. "We're out of here."

The Cadillac backed out of the yard and sped away.

"All right, everybody," Mrs. Hunter said. "Do you all have your cell phones?"

All four girls held up their cell phones. Mr. and Mrs. Hunter hugged Taylor and Kylie.

"Have fun," they said. "We'll miss you."

The girls piled into the car. Kylie and Taylor both went for the driver's seat.

"You always drive," Taylor complained. "I want to drive."

"You will," Kylie promised.

Taylor sighed and took the passenger seat. Then she smiled and waved at her dad, who was videotaping again.

The car's top was down. Kylie started it up. "Ah," she said. "Friends, the winding road, the big blue sky, America."

"Don't forget snowboarding, downhill skiing, aerials—the best athletes in the world," Taylor put in.

Kylie pulled out of the driveway. *"Road trip!"* Jenn cried. *"This is so hype."*

"Are we ready?" Kylie asked.

"Yes!" the other girls called.

"Let's do it!" Kylie pressed the gas pedal and took off down the street. She waved good-bye to her parents. They were on their way!

An hour later they were zooming down the highway. Kylie was in her driving groove. The car almost felt like a part of her. This trip is going to be the greatest, *she thought.*

She glanced at Jenn and Lyndi in the backseat. Lyndi looked miserable, still trying to keep her hair from blowing.

"I know you guys don't care," she complained. "But I'm starting to look like Shaggy."

"Could be worse," Jenn joked. "You could look like Scooby-Doo."

Lyndi pouted. "I hope we don't run into Danny— at least not until I get a chance to brush my hair."

Kylie rolled her eyes. Lyndi was not in the road-trip spirit.

"What do you see in Danny, anyway?" Taylor asked.

"He's hot," Lyndi replied.

"No," Taylor told Lyndi. "This car is hot. And unlike Danny, it's reliable and will take you places."

Kylie's cell phone rang. It was Danny. "Bad news, girls," he told her. "We've—uh—had a little accident."

"An accident!" Kylie cried. "What happened? Are you okay?"

"Yeah, we're fine," Danny said. "But the Caddy's not in such good shape. We ran over some spikes backing into a burrito joint. We've got four flat tires."

Kylie laughed. "I knew it had to be food related. Toast's dad is going to kill you!" she said.

"Nah—he'll probably just kill Toast," Danny said. "Anyway, we're towing the car home. We're going to try to fly to Salt Lake City in the morning. Want to come with us, or meet us there?"

"Hold on." Kylie explained the situation to the other girls. "Now's your chance to fly, Taylor," she added.

"Too late," Taylor said. "The Winter Olympics won't wait for us. We're driving through. I've already missed ice hockey, bobsledding . . ."

"Okay," Kylie said. "Danny—we'll see you guys in Utah." She put away the phone.

"Those guys are so lame," Jenn said.

"Yeah," Kylie agreed. "But the thought of burritos is making me hungry."

"I'm hungry, too," Lyndi added.

"No, no!" Taylor said. "Let's chew up miles, not food."

Kylie spotted a diner up ahead. "Come on, Tay," she prodded. "Food run."

They pulled into the diner and parked. "We'll stop for twenty minutes—that's all," Taylor warned. "Then we're back on the road."

"Twenty minutes," Jenn said. "That means no food that needs to be cooked or chewed. We'll get four bowls of cold milk."

"All right," Taylor agreed. "Twenty-five minutes."

Kylie jumped out of the car. "Taylor, chill. It's smooth sailing from here on in."

They went into the diner and scarfed down some food. Taylor kept an eye on her watch the whole time. Twenty-five minutes later they came out into the parking lot.

"It's amazing how fast you can eat," Jenn said, staring at Taylor, "when someone is timing you."

Kylie scanned the lot for their car. But she couldn't see a Mustang convertible anywhere.

"Taylor," Kylie said. "Where did we park?"

"Right over—" Taylor pointed to a corner of the lot. It was empty. Taylor gasped. "There."

Kylie ran up and down the parking lot, searching for the car. But it had disappeared.

"I don't believe it!" Kylie gasped. "Our car has been stolen!"

chapter three

I wandered into wardrobe on Wednesday afternoon.

"Try this on, Mary-Kate," Christina said. "It's a shirt for one of your Vegas scenes. I sewed on the sequins to brighten it up a little."

I glanced at the sequins at the neckline of the shirt. They added just the right touch to make it look special. "It's beautiful," I said, slipping out of my movie clothes and into my jeans. "But let me go take my makeup off before I put it on."

"Why don't I bring it back to our room," Christina offered. "You can try it on there."

I headed for the makeup room while Christina put away some costumes. Shooting was over for the day, and I couldn't wait to wash off my movie makeup.

For the past few days while I was busy with the movie, Christina had been hanging around the wardrobe room with Amy Burke. She had a good eye for clothes. So good that even Amy had to admit that Christina was a big help to her.

Then, yesterday, Amy made it official and asked Christina to be her assistant!

Jake's parents agreed that it would be okay for Christina to work on the movie with us, so Christina packed her bags and brought them to the set. Later, I'd be showing her to our room in the Orangeview Motel.

Ashley offered to move in with Rachel so Christina could stay with me. I had to admit I was excited to have her—it was kind of like having part of Jake with me.

I felt totally sad when he left for basketball camp, but I was glad we had a chance to say good-bye on our date last night.

I heard voices as I opened the door to the makeup room. Noah was sitting in front of the mirror with Tom, the hairdresser, standing behind him. "I don't want it to look too streaky," Noah said, running his hand through his hair.

He noticed me and stopped talking. "Hi, Mary-Kate," he said, getting up from the chair. He leaned nonchalantly against the counter.

"Hi, guys." I reached for a jar of cold cream and started dabbing away my makeup. In the mirror I could see Tom studying Noah's hair.

"I like the surfer look you've got going on," Tom

27

finally said. "But whoever does your highlights is butchering your hair!"

Highlights? I stared at Noah. He went around telling everyone he got those streaks from the time he spent on his surfboard.

Noah reddened. "Tom," he sputtered. "Who said anything about highlights?"

"*You* did!" Tom insisted. "You came in here and asked me if I thought you should go blonder—"

"Stop joking around," Noah interrupted. He flashed me an embarrassed smile.

I smiled back, trying not to laugh. Noah acted like some big surfboard king. But I would bet he had never caught a wave in his life.

Tom sighed and glanced at me. "Whatever. I'm out of here. See you kids in the morning."

"I've got to go, too," Noah said quickly. "See you, Mary-Kate."

"See you."

As soon as Noah left, I burst out laughing. If only Ashley had been able to see that! She'd be over Noah for good.

"Are you sure Ashley doesn't mind?" Christina asked as I opened the door to our motel room. "I didn't mean to kick her out."

"I'm sure," I promised. "It was her idea. I think Rachel was a little cranky about it, though. She was hoping to have a room all to herself. But why should she? Nobody else does."

Christina laughed. "She's a little stuck-up, isn't she? I could tell just by watching her on the set."

"She's a good actress—she's had a lot of experience," I explained. "But, yeah, she's a little stuck-up."

Christina put away her things. Then we stepped out onto the motel walkway for some air. Our room was on the second floor of the two-story motel. All the rooms were lined up along outdoor walkways surrounding a pool. The restaurant was in a round fifties-style building attached to the motel on the first floor.

Christina angled her face to catch a few rays of late-afternoon sun. I leaned against the railing and watched the people by the pool below us.

"There's Ashley," I said. She was sitting on a pool chair in a bikini top and sarong, talking to Noah. I waved at her, but she didn't see me.

Christina glanced down. "She's with that guy Noah. What do you think of him?"

"Noah?" I studied him. He lounged back in his chair, dark sunglasses shielding his eyes. Ashley was sitting up and leaning toward him, listening while he talked. The sun glistened on his golden hair and shiny dark glasses. I thought about how his hair got that golden sheen and started laughing.

"He's good-looking," I said.

"I guess," Christina agreed. "How do you think he gets his hair to look so good?"

"He highlights it," I told her.

"He does?" Christina gasped. "I thought he seemed kind of vain. I mean, I don't know the guy—I've talked to him only once. But look at the way he's lounging in that chair. He's just so . . . into himself."

I knew what she meant.

"Your sister likes him, doesn't she?" Christina said.

"I think so," I answered. Christina impressed me. She really noticed things.

"I don't get it," Christina said. "Can't she see through his superstar act? He didn't fool you for a second."

I decided to give Ashley the benefit of the doubt. "She knows him better than we do. Maybe she's seen another side of him—"

"Hey, girls. Checking out the action at the pool?" Buddy came out of his room, three doors down from ours with a jumbo bag of tortilla chips in his hand. His blue T-shirt was inside out, and his jeans were covered in crumbs. He strolled down the walkway toward us, stuffing a wad of chips into his mouth.

"Hi, Buddy," I said. "Have you met my friend Christina?"

Buddy chewed and swallowed. "I haven't." He

smiled and nodded at Christina. "But I've been wondering who the mystery girl was."

"Christina's moving to L.A. from New York," I explained.

Buddy made a goofy monster face. "Excellent," he stage-whispered, rubbing his hands together. "Good job, Mary-Kate—you've found us another fresh brain."

"Fresh brain?" Christina asked. "What are you talking about?"

"You haven't told her?" Buddy asked me.

I shrugged. I wasn't sure where he was going with this.

"Haven't you noticed a difference between Californians and easterners?" Buddy asked Christina. "I'll tell you what it is—the sun melts our brains. A few years out here and our brains turn to mush. We need to replace them. That's where you come in. . . ."

He inched toward Christina, reaching for her scalp. She shrank back, laughing.

"Yessss," he hissed. "I'm due for a brain transplant. Let's see what you've got there. . . ."

Christina shrieked and darted away from him, giggling. Buddy dropped the monster character and dug into the bag of tortillas again. "I'm serious," he joked, munching on a few chips. "I wouldn't sleep if I were you." He held out the bag. "Chip?"

"No, thanks," Christina said, still laughing. "Mary-Kate, why didn't you warn me about this?"

"Maybe *I* want your brain, too," I teased.

Buddy leaned against the railing and stared toward the pool. "Is that Ashley down there?" he asked.

"That's Ashley," I told him.

He sighed and ate a few more chips. "And she's talking to Noah, right?"

"Yep," I replied.

He stared at his bag of chips. "Anyone hungry?" he asked. "I've got a toaster oven in my room. I can make nachos."

Christina and I shook our heads. "No, thanks," I said. "It's almost dinnertime."

"Okay." Buddy headed back down the walkway. "If you change your minds, I'll be in my room."

A few minutes later the smell of melting cheese wafted toward us.

"Buddy's funny," Christina said.

"Yeah," I agreed. "And he's really a nice guy. I kind of get the feeling he likes Ashley."

"I think so, too," Christina said. "It's too bad Ashley's all hung up on Mr. Gorgeous."

"You're right," I said. "I mean, sure, Buddy's kind of messy. But if you look beyond that, he's a nice, funny cute guy."

"Some people can't see past the shallow stuff,"

Christina said. "But we see the real Buddy."

Buddy stepped out of his room, a plate of nachos in one hand. Now his T-shirt was right side out, but it was tucked in on one side and untucked on the other. His hair stuck out at all angles, as usual. He turned and waved to us. We waved back.

"Yeah, he's a good guy," I said. "But he could use a little help with his presentation. . . ."

"My mom really wants me to go to college," Noah said to me. "But what's the point? You know what I mean, Ashley?"

"I'm looking forward to college," I told him.

"Sure, maybe college is good for you," he said. "But I want to be an actor. A movie star! And I'm ready to go. College would just be a waste of time for me."

The cast was having dinner together at a big round table in the Orangeview restaurant. I glanced across the table at Mary-Kate. Christina was whispering to her and giggling.

They've been doing that all night, I thought, annoyed. *What are they whispering about?*

"My parents keep saying I need something to fall back on in case the acting thing doesn't work out," Noah went on. "But I already know how to play the guitar, right? So I can always be a rock star."

"I love acting, too," I said. "But I think you can

learn things in college that will make you a better actor. Like studying the great plays."

Across the table, Christina and Mary-Kate giggled. I felt my face turn red. For a second I wondered, *Are they laughing at me?*

Then I shook my head. *Who cares what Christina and Mary-Kate are whispering about,* I thought. *This is fun. Noah is sitting next to me—he made a point of it—and now he's telling me about his hopes and dreams.*

Buddy sat on my other side, a big plate of meat loaf and mashed potatoes in front of him.

"I've got to save room for dessert," he told me. "The banana cream pie is killer here."

I laughed. "I'll definitely try some." *He's just like Toast,* I thought. *Talk about typecasting.*

After dinner, Noah pulled me aside. "You want to go for a walk?" he suggested. "I want to ask you something."

"Sure." *A walk with Noah alone?* I thought. *Great!*

We left the restaurant and strolled around the pool.

"I've been thinking about the script," Noah told me. "My character, Sam, has the hots for Kylie, right?"

I nodded. "Right." I played it cool, but inside I

was bursting with happiness. *This is so exciting!* I thought. *We're two actors, working on a movie together. And we're discussing the script! How awesome is this?*

"Kylie resists Sam," Noah went on. "It's pretty clear she doesn't like him. But I keep thinking about your character, Taylor."

"What about her?" I asked.

"I think that Taylor secretly likes Sam. It's in the script if you read between the lines."

"Really?" I hadn't noticed that before. But maybe I'd missed it. "I'll ask the director about that."

"I think you should play Taylor as if she likes Sam—that way Sam won't look so bad in the end. I mean, Sam is a cool guy, right? It makes sense that at least *one* of the girls would like him."

"I'll think about it," I promised. We stopped and lingered in a beam of moonlight. Noah flashed me his dazzling smile.

He wants me to act as if I secretly like him? I thought, melting. *Not a problem. And it wouldn't exactly be acting.*

chapter four

"Mary-Kate, you would have died," Christina said. "It was so funny."

She was lying on top of her bed in our room, telling me about an argument she'd overheard between Rachel and Kip. Dinner was long over, and we'd spent the whole evening hanging out in our room together.

"So Rachel said, 'Listen to me, Kip—I know what I'm talking about. You have to *e-nun-ci-ate.*'" Christina imitated Rachel's crisp voice. "And Kip said, 'Chill out. Stop bossing me around! I'm not going to do that. I don't want to sound all princessy like you!'"

I laughed. Christina mimicked Kip's slow drawl perfectly.

"So then Rachel stamped her foot and said, 'I'm only trying to help!'" Christina finished. "Kip's right—she really is princessy."

"It's true," I agreed. "But she means well." I stood up and started brushing my hair. "I guess I'll get ready for bed," I said. "You can stay up and read for a while if you want, though. The light won't bother me."

"What?" Christina jumped to her feet. "Wait a minute. It's only ten o'clock! You can't go to bed yet."

"I've got to get up really early tomorrow," I explained. "I've got a six A.M. makeup call—and I still have some lines to learn."

"Come on," Christina protested. "It's acting! How hard could it be?"

"It's pretty hard if you don't know your lines," I told her.

"You can go over them in the morning while they do your makeup," Christina said. "I just got here. I want to have some fun. Let's go out!"

I stared at her. "We can't go out," I explained. "We're not supposed to leave the motel after ten without permission. Everybody under eighteen has a curfew."

"So?" Christina scoffed. "Even Jake's parents would let me stay out later than that. What's the point of being here on our own if we can't do what we want?"

"Well, I'm here because I'm working," I replied. "And I don't want to get into trouble."

"No one will find out," Christina insisted. "I heard about this really cool club not far from here. We can go dancing. I haven't been out once since I got to California! Please, Mary-Kate?"

"It sounds like fun, Christina, but we really can't."

"Come on," Christina coaxed. "Your cute little Mustang is just sitting out back in the parking lot, waiting to take us for a ride. . . ."

It was tempting, but I knew it was a bad idea. "I'm sorry. Maybe we can go out another night if we ask permission first. . . ."

Christina shrugged. "Suit yourself, but I'm going dancing tonight, with or without you." She jumped up and changed into a short disco dress.

"You're going alone?" I asked. "How are you going to get there? Taxi?"

Christina laughed. "Taxi? Too expensive. I'll hitchhike."

"Hitchhike!" I yelped. "No way! You can't do that. It's dangerous!"

"Last chance," Christina taunted, snatching up her bag. She started for the door.

I bit my lip. I couldn't let her hitchhike. What if something happened to her? I mean, she was Jake's cousin! I was kind of responsible for her.

"Christina, stop!" I cried.

She paused at the door.

I sighed. "Just . . . let me get my car keys."

"Excellent!" Christina grinned and crossed the room. She threw open my closet and pulled out a sparkly top. "Here." She tossed the top at me. "Put that on over your jeans and we're ready to go!"

"We're not staying out late," I warned her. I changed quickly and we slipped outside to the parking lot.

I unlocked the Mustang, then hesitated. "We can't start the car. Ashley will hear it for sure," I whispered. "She's got eagle ears."

"Okay," Christina said. "You steer and I'll push."

I got into the driver's seat and turned on the headlights. I shifted into neutral and Christina pushed the car into the street. Then I started the engine.

Christina hopped into the front seat. "Let's go!"

We roared off down the road. It felt great to be driving again. After a mile or two, Christina pointed out a blinking neon sign that said "Smash." "That's the place I heard about," she told me. "It's a teen club—strictly under twenty-one."

I turned into the parking lot. It was packed with cars.

"This place is pretty hopping for a Wednesday night," Christina noted.

I had to admit it looked like fun. We parked and headed for the entrance. A burly doorman let us in.

It was dark inside the club and the music was

so loud it made my teeth rattle. Soon my eyes adjusted to the dark. The dance floor was packed with sweaty, wriggling bodies.

"Come on!" Christina shouted in my ear. "Let's get out there!"

We ran onto the dance floor and started moving to the pounding beat. The sound shifted from the latest dance hit to a pop song I'd loved when I was seven years old. Christina was a great dancer, but she was so wild, people had to clear a circle around her.

"This deejay is excellent!" I yelled to her.

"He's great!" she shouted back. "Try this!" She showed me a few dance steps. *Step, clap, step, turn.* I watched her feet move, then practiced the steps until I had them down perfectly. The two of us danced side by side, mirroring each other. *Step, clap, step, turn.*

A girl my age stood next to me and started copying the steps. Then three more kids joined us. Soon a long line snaked across the dance floor. Everybody danced together, following Christina's lead.

"This is so much fun!" I whooped when the deejay speeded up the beat.

"Let's hear it for our line dancers out there!" the deejay called over the P.A. system. The room erupted in cheers and clapping. "Give us some of that disco spirit!" He put on an old disco classic.

The dancers shouted their approval. More and more people joined our line.

"This was my mom's favorite song in high school!" Christina told me.

I laughed. "It was my mom's favorite song, too!"

We danced until we dripped with sweat. The deejay slowed down the music and our dance line began to break up. "Let's snag a couple of bottles of water," Christina suggested.

"Good idea." We headed for the bar.

"You two really set this place on fire." I turned around to see two guys standing behind us. They looked about eighteen or nineteen. One was tall and thin and preppy-looking with straight blond hair. The second one was shorter and cuter with dark blond curls.

"Where did you learn to dance like that?" the cuter one asked, looking at me.

"She taught me." I nodded toward Christina, who was gulping down water.

"I used to live in New York," she said. "I went out dancing all the time. Mostly on school nights."

The guys laughed. "I'm James," the cute one said. "And this is Nick."

We introduced ourselves.

"You girls up for more dancing?" Nick asked.

"Always." Christina took his hand. James and I followed them onto the dance floor.

We danced to a few songs. Nick was a dorky dancer, but James wasn't bad, for a guy. He grabbed my hand and twirled me around. "You're cute," he told me.

"Thanks," I said. I knew he was flirting with me, and I wasn't sure how much to flirt back. I didn't want to be rude, but I wasn't interested in him. I wished Jake was there to dance with me instead.

"Come on." James took my hand as a song ended. "I'll buy you a Coke."

Nick and Christina joined us at the bar. The crowd on the dance floor was beginning to thin out. "This place is beat," Nick said. "You girls want to take a ride? We know about a warehouse party that's probably just getting started now."

Christina said, "Sounds cool," but I caught a glimpse of Nick's watch and cried, "It's almost one A.M.!"

"Yeah." James put his arm around me. "Time to start the real partying."

"I've got to get up in four and a half hours," I said. "Christina, we've got to go back to the motel."

"Where are you staying?" Nick asked. "We'll come with you."

"No!" I said.

Christina pulled me aside. "Come on, Mary-Kate. Let's go to the party," she whispered. "Just for an hour. We might not get another chance like this!"

"Christina—"

"Besides, the cute one likes you!" Christina said.

"Christina!" I cried. "I'm going out with Jake. Remember him? Your cousin?"

"Jake schmake." Christina waved this away. "I won't tell if you won't."

I glanced over at the boys. They were having a conference of their own. Probably plotting to convince us to go with them, I thought.

"Christina, I'm sorry. But we don't know these guys, and I have to go to bed." I fumbled through my purse until I found my car keys. "Right now. We're leaving."

I started toward the exit. "Bye, guys," I said as we passed Nick and James.

"Girls—wait!" James called. They trotted after us and walked us to my car.

Christina and I got into the car and I started the engine. "Will we see you again?" Nick asked.

Christina glanced at me. I shook my head.

"Unlikely," Christina told him. "Sorry, boys!"

I pulled out of the parking space and zoomed away. Christina waved at the boys as they watched us go.

"That was fun," Christina said as we pulled into the motel lot. "Wasn't it worth sneaking out for?"

"The dancing was fun," I admitted. I carefully opened the car door, got out, and shut the door as quietly as I could. "Try not to make any noise," I whispered to Christina.

She nodded. We tiptoed up the concrete stairs to the second floor of the motel. We padded down the walkway. I slowly turned the key in the lock and opened the door. It closed behind us with a soft *click*.

Christina and I collapsed on our beds, giggling. "We did it!" she whispered. "We didn't get caught!"

I glanced at my alarm clock. It was almost two in the morning. "Now I've *really* got to go to sleep," I said. "I'm going to be exhausted tomorrow."

I headed toward the bathroom to brush my teeth. Suddenly there was a knock at the door. I froze.

Christina and I locked eyes. I gulped.

The knock came again, louder this time.

My heart fluttered in my chest. *Oh, no!* I thought. *We're in big trouble now.*

chapter five

"**W**ho do you think it is?" Christina whispered.

"I don't know," I whispered back. I hoped it wasn't Don Maneri, the director of the movie. What if he fired me?

Knock knock knock. "Mary-Kate!" a voice whispered through the door. "I know you're awake!"

I relaxed. "It's Ashley." I crossed the room and opened the door. Ashley, in her pajamas, pushed her way inside and shut the door behind her.

"I knew that was you!" she cried. "That was our car that just pulled into the parking lot, wasn't it? Where were you all night?"

"Ashley, calm down," Christina said. "We just went out for a little fun. It's no big deal."

"No big deal!" Ashley echoed. "We've got a ten o'clock curfew. *And* a six A.M. makeup call! Do you know what time it is?"

"Ashley, you're right," I admitted. "I'm sorry.

And I promise that we won't ever do it again."

Ashley frowned. She cast a suspicious glance at Christina, who lounged against the pillows on her bed and yawned.

"All right." Ashley opened the door. "I'll see you in a few hours," she whispered, shutting the door gently behind her.

"It's amazing," Christina said. "You're so much cooler than Ashley. How can two sisters be so different?"

"Well, we are different," I told her. "But maybe not as different as you think."

"What do you think we are?" Sam asked Kylie. "I mean, like, how would you classify us?"

They were sitting on a bench in Kylie's parents' backyard. Sam reached for Kylie's hand. She struggled to think of an answer to his odd question.

"Umm . . . American teenagers?" she ventured.

Sam shook his head. "No—I mean us. You and me. As a couple."

Kylie glanced down at his hand on top of hers. Why was he pressuring her like this? "Hmm," she began. "Well, I'd say we're friends. Friends is good."

"I'd kind of like to be more." Sam leaned in close to her. Kylie pushed him firmly away. "Sam. I'd say we're in a gray area. Friends, but . . . well, friends."

"Gray?" Sam protested. "I don't think gray is a

real color. Blue, green, yellow, red—those are colors."

"I'm not really ready for blue, green, or any of the so-called real colors," Kylie said. Get it? she thought.

"Okay, fine." Sam pulled away from her. "But does it have to be gray? Gray is sort of blah."

Kylie sighed. "All right. We'll call it charcoal, okay? We're in a charcoal area. . . ."

Sam frowned. Kylie glanced across the yard. The road trip was on hold for a day, since the girls' car had been stolen and the boys had blown out the tires on their Cadillac. So the Hunters decided to throw a barbecue. Kylie's dad was busy grilling steaks, surrounded by Taylor and their other friends.

Kylie stood up. "Speaking of charcoal—let's go see how the steaks are doing." She hurried to the grill, Sam at her heels.

Mrs. Hunter brought out a tray of appetizers and a large pitcher of lemonade. Taylor helped her pass out the appetizers to Jenn, Lyndi, Danny, and Toast.

Toast hovered near the grill, watching the steaks cook.

"Fresh lemonade," he said, taking a glass from Mrs. Hunter. "Nice touch, Mrs. H." He grabbed three stuffed mushrooms from the tray and popped them into his mouth.

Mr. Hunter eyed him. "Toast—these steaks are USDA prime. Treat them carefully."

"No prob, Mr. H.," Toast mumbled with his

mouth full. "I have the utmost respect for meat."

"The steaks look great, Dad," Taylor said.

Mr. Hunter waved his spatula. "Steak is a once-in-a-while thing, but when you do it . . ."

"Do it right," Mrs. Hunter finished.

"The lemonade is excellent, too," Toast put in. "Jenn, let me get you some."

Toast reached for the lemonade pitcher on the picnic table next to the grill. Danny grinned slyly. He nudged Toast and Toast fell forward—knocking the pitcher into the air. Lyndi shrieked. Lemonade rained down on the steaks. The fire sputtered and fizzled out.

Everyone groaned and glared at Toast. "The steaks are ruined!" Lyndi cried.

"Maybe not." Toast backed away as his friends angrily surrounded him. "Steak marinated in lemonade—it could be interesting."

Taylor sighed. "I'll call for Chinese."

Toast scraped the last bit of kung pao chicken from the bottom of a carton of Chinese food. Kylie picked at an egg roll. The Chinese food was almost gone. Kylie, Taylor, and their friends relaxed on the Hunters' front porch.

"Thanks for having us over, you guys," Danny said to Kylie and Taylor.

"Next time we'll cook waterproof meat," Kylie joked.

Toast pointed to Danny. "He pushed me."

Danny put on his most innocent face. "Who, me?"

"Save the bickering for tomorrow," Taylor said. "We've got to get to sleep. Our bus leaves at eight in the morning."

Since they couldn't drive to Salt Lake City, they had tried to book a flight. But all the flights from Los Angeles were full. They had no choice now but to take the bus to Las Vegas and fly from there.

"Eight o'clock," Danny said. "We're there." The boys started down the walk. The girls followed them to the edge of the yard. Sam leaned toward Kylie for a kiss. She angled her face away. His lips brushed her cheek.

"I guess charcoal's pretty cool—for now," Sam said.

"Yo, Tay, what are you reading about?" Danny tapped on the ski magazine Taylor was reading.

They were settled on a Greyhound headed for Las Vegas. The bus was only half full, so they had plenty of room to spread out. Danny sat next to Taylor. Lyndi had a seat to herself. Jenn and Toast sat in the back with Sam and Kylie directly behind them.

Taylor lowered the magazine. "I'm reading about Picabo Street. She is way cool. Gold in the Super G in 1998 and silver in the 1994 downhill. I can't wait to see her ski."

"Oh." Danny nodded.

Taylor went back to her magazine. She loved skiing. Soon I'll be at the Olympics! *she thought. She couldn't believe it. She'd get to see Picabo Street—and, even better, Alex Reisher—in person!*

"Peek-a-boo." Danny peeked at her under her magazine. Taylor tried to ignore him.

"Peek-a-boo," Danny repeated.

Annoyed, Taylor put down the magazine. "Danny—what?"

"Don't you get it?" Danny asked. "Peek-a-boo—Picabo Street."

Across the aisle, Lyndi cracked up. "I get it! That's funny."

Taylor sighed. Danny's joke wasn't the least bit funny. She wished Lyndi wouldn't encourage him. . . . And then something struck her. Danny . . . and Lyndi . . .

"You know, I just had an inspiration," Taylor said. "You two would make a perfect couple!"

"Really?" Lyndi squealed.

"Really . . ." Danny looked as if he might be sick.

It's too bad Danny doesn't see how sweet Lyndi is, *Taylor thought.* Because Lyndi is so crazy about him—and I'm definitely not.

She stood, picked up her magazine, and brushed past Danny. "I think I'll move to that empty seat up there," she said, pointing a row ahead. "So I can stretch out a little."

Taylor settled across the aisle from Jenn and Toast. They were munching on bagels. Taylor tried to read her magazine but her ears perked up when she heard Jenn and Toast talking.

"Is Danny your best friend?" Jenn asked Toast.

"Since sixth grade," Toast replied. "Why?"

Taylor hid her face behind her magazine, but she couldn't help leaning closer to listen. What was Jenn getting at?

"Well, we girls make fun of each other," Jenn explained. "But it's in a harmless, fun way. We don't try to embarrass each other or anything like that."

"Yeah?" Toast said. "That's good."

"But Danny likes to make you the butt of his jokes," Jenn went on. "And they're sort of mean jokes."

Taylor glanced across the aisle to see how Toast was taking this. Toast looked solemn and thoughtful.

"I didn't mean to get all heavy, Toast," Jenn added. "It's just something I've been noticing."

Toast nodded. "Yeah. Me, too." He smiled at Jenn. "By the way, my real name is Joshua."

A couple of hours later the bus pulled into a depot. Taylor stared out the window at the small desert town. Next to the depot was a diner.

"Anybody hungry?" Taylor asked.

"I am," Danny said.

"Me, too," Lyndi piped up.

Kylie, Sam, Toast, and Jenn were curled up in the back of the bus, sleeping. Taylor picked up her backpack and started down the aisle toward them.

"Hey." She poked Kylie. "Want some lunch?"

Kylie sleepily lifted her head. She mumbled something, and waved Taylor away.

"Suit yourself," Taylor said. She followed Danny and Lyndi off the bus and into the diner.

After a quick lunch, Taylor, Danny, and Lyndi boarded the bus. Taylor glanced toward the back. She saw a few bodies huddled under a pile of coats.

"I can't believe they're still sleeping," she said.

"Especially Toast," Danny added. "It's not like him to skip a meal."

They sat down and the bus took off. Danny and Lyndi soon fell asleep. Taylor lost herself in her ski magazine. When she finally looked up the bus was pulling into another depot.

"Last stop, Baker," the bus driver announced. "This is Baker. End of the line."

"End of the line?" Taylor cried. She stared out the window at the tiniest town she'd ever seen. There was a small general store, a one-pump gas station, and a diner surrounded by desert.

"This isn't Vegas." She gasped.

Danny and Lyndi sat up. "Where are we?" Lyndi asked.

"I can't believe this!" Taylor cried. "We must be on

the wrong bus!" She turned toward the back of the bus. "Kylie!" she called. But Kylie wasn't there! Neither were Sam, Toast, or Jenn!

"Okay, kids," the bus driver said. "Everybody off. This is the last stop."

"Oh, no!" Taylor cried. "We're definitely on the wrong bus! Now we're lost!"

"Cut!" Don called out when Ashley finished her line. "Good work, kids. That's it for today."

Finally, I thought, dropping my head into my hands. I was exhausted. We'd been shooting all day, and it felt like the longest day of my life. *I'll never stay out late again,* I vowed.

"Hey, Mary-Kate." Buddy tapped me on the shoulder. "We're all meeting at the coffee shop if you want to have dinner."

"Thanks, Buddy." I wasn't sure I'd make it. I was almost too tired to eat.

That morning the makeup artist had to spend extra time covering up the circles under my eyes. And I flubbed my lines a couple of times, which was really upsetting. It wasn't like me at all.

"Mary-Kate—are you feeling all right?" Buddy asked.

"Yeah, I'm fine," I told him. I could see the concern in his eyes. "I'm just a little tired. But thanks for asking."

"Can I get you a milk shake or something?" Buddy offered. "When I'm tired, nothing peps me up like a milk shake."

I laughed. "No thanks. I think I'll just lie down for a while."

"Hey, everybody!" Don shouted. "Don't forget— we're leaving for Las Vegas in the morning to shoot the Nevada scenes. Everybody be up and ready to go by seven. All right, that's it."

I headed for the door. I couldn't wait to lie down. But then Don called out, "Mary-Kate? Can I see you for a minute?"

Oh, no! I thought. *He found out that I sneaked out last night. Or he thought I was terrible today. Something's wrong. He's going to fire me!*

chapter six

I tried to look calm even though I was shaking inside. Why would Don want to talk to me? It had to be something bad.

"Hey, Mary-Kate," Don said. "Listen—I was talking to Amy, and she told me Christina has been working with her on the costumes."

"Yes?" Had Christina done something wrong? Was she in trouble?

"Anyway, Amy says Christina's been a lot of help," Don went on. I relaxed a little. "If she wants to come along with us to Las Vegas and Park City, she's welcome. Will you tell her for me?"

"Sure!" I waited a few seconds to see if he wanted anything else.

"Thanks, Mary-Kate." Don walked away and started talking to a cameraman.

Whew! I wasn't in trouble after all. I hurried out of the soundstage, opened the door, and stepped into the bright sunshine. Ashley was waiting for me, arms folded across her chest, frowning. She didn't look happy.

"What did Don want?" Ashley asked as we walked toward the motel.

"He just wanted to let me know that Christina can come with us to Las Vegas if she wants."

"Great." Ashley sighed. "Mary-Kate—maybe nobody else noticed how tired you were today—but I did. And I'm worried about you! It's not like you to break the rules like that."

"I know," I admitted. "But it's not as if anything terrible happened. I'll get a good night's sleep tonight. I promise."

"I wish Christina weren't going with us on the road," Ashley said. "I think she's a bad influence on you."

"What?" I stopped short and whirled around to face her. "What are you talking about?"

"It was her idea to go out last night, wasn't it?" Ashley said. "You never would have done that without her."

"Well—it *was* her idea," I admitted. "She told me she was going to go out by herself if I didn't go with her."

I let out a sigh. "Ashley—don't worry about me. I can take care of myself." I turned and walked away.

I didn't need Ashley to mother me—Mom was good at that already. But, inside, part of me agreed with her. I wished I hadn't stayed out so late the night before. It definitely wasn't worth it.

I watched Mary-Kate walk away. What was the matter with her? Why was she acting this way? No matter what she said, I *was* worried about her.

Something about Christina just didn't seem right to me. *Does Mary-Kate really like her?* I wondered. *Or is she defending her just because she's Jake's cousin?*

"I think you'll like this next song, Ashley," Noah said to me. "It's in honor of the greatest rock and roll star of all time—Mr. Elvis Presley." He sat near me at the back of the van, strumming his guitar.

"And Vegas," Buddy added. "Don't forget Vegas, baby."

Our van zoomed down the highway on the road to Las Vegas, crammed with most of the cast of *Getting There*. Mary-Kate and Christina sat near the front. Kip, Rachel, Delia, and Buddy surrounded me and Noah.

"All right!" I cheered. "Las Vegas!" I was so excited to get there. I couldn't believe that soon we'd be working on location—especially when the location was a cool place like Vegas!

"Have you been to Las Vegas before, Noah?" Delia asked.

"No," Noah admitted. "But I know it's hip and swinging."

"Dude, I went there once with my grandmother," Kip said. "It was nothing but old people for miles around. Old people playing slot machines."

"Maybe your grandmother doesn't know the hot spots," Rachel suggested.

Kip bristled. "Are you saying my grandma's not cool?"

"Well," Rachel began. "I don't know your grandmother, but—"

"Does anybody want to hear this song?" Noah interrupted. "Or are we going to sit here all day talking about Kip's grandma?"

"I want to hear it," I said. Noah crinkled his blue eyes at me and started playing "Viva Las Vegas." When it was over, everyone in the van clapped and whistled.

"Thank you, thank you very much," Noah drawled in an Elvis voice. "Man, Elvis is the greatest." He played another Elvis song, "Jailhouse Rock." We all bounced along with the music.

"Now play my favorite," Buddy requested. "'Love Me Tender.'"

"I've got something else in mind," Noah said.

"My friend is in a band and he wrote this song. It's called 'Paisley Girl.' It might not be as good as an Elvis song—but maybe you'll like it." He grinned at me and started singing:

> *I love that girl with the pretty blond hair*
> *The girl who makes me stop and stare*
> *Oh, Paisley, that Paisley girl.*

It was a really good song. Noah was watching me as he sang—singing it to me!

> *She's the girl who makes my heart beat*
> *She's the music that moves my feet*
> *Oh, Ashley, that Ashley girl.*

I smiled broadly. Noah changed the words! Now he really *was* singing the song just for me!

Everyone was swaying and clapping along with the song—everyone except for Mary-Kate and Christina. Christina leaned close to Mary-Kate and whispered something in her ear.

What is with her? I wondered. *Is she making fun of Noah's song? What's her problem?*

I decided then and there that I definitely did *not* like Christina. And I wished Mary-Kate didn't hang out with her so much!

But . . . what could I do about it?

• • •

"Do you believe this guy?" Christina whispered in my ear. Noah was singing a song, changing the words to fit Ashley's name in. "He thinks he's the coolest thing since the iceberg that hit the *Titanic*."

I nodded and watched Ashley. She sat close to Noah, beaming. *Why does she like him so much?* I wondered. *Can't she see how phony he is?*

"Inside, he's a total jerk," Christina added. "He'll do anything for attention. I'll bet he'd wear a gorilla suit if he thought it would make him a star."

I giggled, but I felt a little guilty. I didn't think it was nice of us to talk about Noah when he was sitting only four feet away. I knew he couldn't hear us, but still . . .

At the same time, I thought Christina was right. I felt kind of embarrassed for Ashley. She looked so happy that Noah was singing her name. But did that mean he really liked her? Or was he just showing off?

Buddy sat on her other side, being a good sport. But Ashley ignored him.

The van veered onto an exit ramp and stopped at a rest area. "We're stopping for gas," the driver told us. "Anybody want to get out and stretch their legs?"

"Definitely." Christina groaned. We'd been on the road for four hours. We all stumbled out of the van and wandered over to the convenience store for snacks.

Christina and I bought iced teas and leaned against the van while it gassed up. A shiny red Ferrari sports car pulled up on the other side of the gas pump.

"Wow!" Christina gasped. "Look at that car."

The car gleamed in the sun, its top down. A man hopped out of the car and hurried into the convenience store.

"Those buttery leather seats are calling out for me," Christina whispered. "And look—he left he keys in the ignition."

"So?" I said.

Christina glanced at the convenience store. The man had disappeared inside.

"Come on, Mary-Kate," she said. "The line's really long. He'll be in there forever."

"What are you doing?" I asked. She walked up to the sports car and jumped inside! She settled behind the wheel and reached for the ignition.

"Mary-Kate, get in!" She waved frantically at me. "Hurry! Let's go for a ride!"

chapter seven

"Christina, are you crazy?" I asked. I hurried over to the car and tried to pull her out. "Get out of there!"

The owner of the Ferrari suddenly burst out of the store and ran toward us. "What do you think you're doing?" he yelled. "Get out of my car!"

Christina laughed and hopped out of the car. "Don't freak," she said to the man. "I just wanted to see how it felt to sit in a cool car like yours. I wasn't going to *steal* it or anything." She laughed again. "Sorry. I didn't mean to upset you."

The man frowned. "All right," he said, getting into the car and starting it up. "I guess there's no harm done."

"Bye!" Christina called. With a screech of its tires the Ferrari roared away.

The others started piling back into the van. "You should have gotten into the car with me!" Christina whispered. "We could have been long gone by now!"

I stared at her. Was she serious?

"Lighten up, Mary-Kate," Christina said. "I'm just fooling around."

I breathed a sigh of relief as we joined the others in the van. Christina didn't really do any harm, I told myself. So why was I so freaked out?

The guitar started up in the back of the van and soon Noah was singing again. "Ugh." Christina groaned. "Will he ever stop?"

"Noah is so into you, Ashley," Rachel said. We were settling into our hotel room in Las Vegas that evening. I was sharing with Rachel and Delia. Mary-Kate and Christina were next door in a double.

"Do you think so?" I asked. I knew Noah was paying some attention to me, but I wasn't sure why. Sometimes he seemed to like me, but other times he seemed kind of self-centered.

"I think it's pretty obvious," Delia agreed. "Changing the words to that song the way he did? He didn't say anything about 'Delia girl.'"

"Or 'Rachel girl.'" Rachel sighed. "He's so cute."

"If Noah likes me so much, why doesn't he ask me out?" I asked. It was something that had been bothering me. Sure, Noah flirted with me all the time—but he never took it one step further.

"Maybe he doesn't know you like him," Delia

suggested. "Maybe he needs a little push."

"Maybe you should do something to show him how you feel about him," Rachel said.

"Like what?" I asked.

"Well, let's think." Delia sat down on her bed. "What does Noah like?"

"He loves music," Rachel said. "Are you a good singer, Ashley?"

"I'm not bad," I admitted.

"And Elvis," Delia added. "He's into Elvis Presley."

"Hey, have you guys spotted any Elvis impersonators yet?" Rachel asked. "I love those guys! They're so funny!"

"There are two of them in our movie," Delia said. "Buddy's playing one."

"That's it!" I cried. "It's perfect! It combines everything Noah likes—all in one package!"

"What?" Rachel asked. "What are you talking about?"

"Elvis impersonators!" I told her. "I'll send Noah an Elvis-gram—only *I'll* be the singing Elvis! I'll get one of the spare costumes from the wardrobe room. It will be perfect!"

"Girl, you're brave," Rachel said.

"But if you can pull it off, you'll be a hit," Delia added. "And he'll definitely know how you feel."

My mind was humming with plans. *I'll be a great Elvis!* I thought. *And Noah will love it.*

• • •

"*Where could they be?*" *Kylie cried. She woke up on the bus and found herself riding along the Strip in Las Vegas, past neon signs and glittery casinos and hotels. But when she looked around the bus she couldn't find Taylor, Danny, or Lyndi anywhere!*

Kylie rummaged through her bag and found her cell phone. "I've got to call Taylor," she said. "Maybe something happened to her!"

She dialed Taylor's number, but nothing happened. "There's no signal!" she wailed.

Sam grabbed Kylie's arm and pulled her into her seat. "I'm sure Taylor is okay," he said.

"She's probably back at that depot," Jenn said.

"Yeah," Toast agreed. "They must have missed the bus or something. I'm sure they're fine."

But Kylie couldn't stop shaking. What if they were lost? What if something happened to them? "I'd better call my parents," she said.

She started to dial, but Sam put his hand over the phone. "Kylie—if your parents hear about another screw-up—after our tires being punctured and your car getting stolen—what are they going to do? My guess is—trip over."

Kylie sighed. Sam was right. Her parents were pretty cool—but they could take only so much.

"All right," she said. "I'll calm down. I'll just keep calling Taylor until I reach her." And it had

better be soon, *she thought.* Or that's the end of this road trip.

"I can't reach Kylie," Taylor said. She stood in front of the Baker general store with Danny and Lyndi, frantically dialing her cell phone. "There's no reception out here! She must be in Vegas, freaking."

"At least Vegas is on a map." Danny stared at the tiny town while a tumbleweed bounded by. "This town is so small, Mini-me wouldn't fit in it."

Lyndi laughed, but Taylor glared at Danny. "We screwed up majorly," she said. "I don't think this is the time for funny."

Danny shrugged. "What else is there to do but laugh?"

Taylor frowned. "I can't reach Kylie, the next bus to Vegas leaves in six hours, the only motel is a campground tent with a complimentary snake, and if I call my parents, our trip is history. Do you still think this is funny?"

"You're right," Danny agreed. "This isn't funny."

"All I wanted was to go to the Winter Olympics," Taylor sighed.

"There's always two thousand six," Lyndi put in.

"In Turin, Italy," Taylor snapped.

"Let's check out the diner," Danny suggested.

"You go," Taylor said. "I think I need to be alone for a minute."

Danny and Lyndi headed off to the diner. Taylor settled on the bumper of a motor home parked in front of the general store. Why is this happening? *she thought.* Why won't anything go right on this trip? Will I ever get to the Olympics?

From inside the store, she heard someone playing an old song on the piano. The wind picked up and blew dust in her face. She stood up, coughing, and brushing the dust from her eyes. Then her cell phone rang—and it was the most beautiful sound she'd ever heard!

"Kylie!" *Taylor cried, answering the phone.* "I've been trying to call you!"

"What happened to you?" *Kylie asked.* "Where are you?"

"We're in Baker, California," *Taylor replied.* "Otherwise known as the capital of nowhere."

"We're in Las Vegas," *Kylie told her.* "You're okay, right? Because I've been sort of freaking."

"Me, too," *Taylor admitted.* "But we're fine, Kylie. We just have to find a way to get to you."

"What can we do?" *Kylie asked.*

"Just stay put," *Taylor said.*

"Hey—I almost called Mom and Dad," *Kylie said.* "What about you?"

"Came close, but no," *Taylor said.* "I figure, I got myself into this mess, I'll get myself out. We'll hook up with you in Vegas and fly to Utah. I promise."

"When can you get here?" *Kylie asked.*

"I'm not sure yet," Taylor said. "I'll let you know. Just stay there and wait for us."

"We will," Kylie promised.

Taylor clicked off and closed her phone, feeling much better. At least now she knew where everyone was and that they were all right.

She climbed the three steps into the general store. A few old men sat around a card table, drinking soda and playing checkers. A girl about Taylor's age played an old upright piano. She wore dirty overalls over a torn white T-shirt and old sneakers. She smiled at Taylor. *She's cute,* Taylor thought, admiring the girl's long, straight brown hair and friendly brown eyes. *And she's a very good musician.*

Taylor bought a Coke and sat down near the piano to listen. A few minutes later the girl stopped playing.

"Hi," she said. "I'm Charly."

"I'm Taylor."

"You're either a mirage, or you're lost," Charly ventured. "Because I never see anyone my age around here."

Taylor grinned. "I'm real all right."

"Then how'd you end up here?" Charly asked.

Tears sprang to Taylor's eyes. It was all so frustrating! She shook her head, unable to speak for a second.

"I'm sorry," Charly said. "None of my business."

"It's okay," Taylor said, and the story began to

pour out of her. "All I wanted was to go to the Olympics. I don't think that's asking too much. I mean, I worked my butt off to get the tickets."

The old men stopped their checkers game to listen to Taylor's story.

"I should have just gone by myself," Taylor went on. "But no, I had to make it a group thing with my sister and friends. And, my luck, this is the group that can do absolutely nothing right."

"What happened?" one of the old men asked.

"My awesome car was stolen," Taylor explained. "The boys' Caddy got spiked, all the flights were booked, Buddy spilled lemonade all over the steaks, we got on the wrong bus, we're one hundred and twenty miles from Vegas, the Olympics are almost over, I thought I lost my sister, and thankfully some good news—I found my sister."

"That's the saddest story ever," Charly said.

"Probably not," Taylor said. "But it's in the top ten."

Charly brightened. "I know—I'll take you to Vegas."

"No," Taylor protested. "I can't impose on you like that."

"Please, Taylor," Charly insisted. "I never get to hang with anyone my age. It will be fun!"

"After all the bad luck I've had you really want to hang with me?"

Charly nodded. "Your luck is about to change."

• • •

"Well," Kylie said. "We've got some time to kill before the others get here. What should we do?"

"Yeah," Sam agreed. "Let's hit the town."

"Let's eat!" Toast added.

They headed for Fremont Street, where all the big casinos were clustered. They grabbed sandwiches at the first deli they saw and ate them while they walked. Kylie blinked at all the flashing neon signs. "Want to see a show tonight?" she asked the others. "How about Cirque du Soleil?"

"Sold out," Sam told her.

"Buffet," Toast suggested.

"Toast—you just had a sandwich," Jenn protested.

"So?" Toast said. "That's just a snack. I'm ready for a meal. A real meal."

"Chill," Jenn told him. "We'll eat again later."

"How about Siegfried and Roy?" Kylie asked.

"Sold out," Sam announced.

"Buffet," Toast repeated.

A strange man approached them. "Young people," he said in an Indian accent. "I am Raj. You could be very good witnesses."

"He's going to commit a crime!" Jenn cried.

Raj shook his head. "No no no. Witnesses to a wedding." He pointed to a tiny wedding chapel on the corner.

"A real wedding?" Sam asked.

Raj nodded. "Bride, groom, rice . . ."

"Would that rice be fried or white?" Toast asked.

"I'll treat, you-eat-all buffet," Raj promised. "If you will be the witnesses."

"Yes!" Toast cheered. "Excellent! You are the man!"

Kylie shrugged. "Well, we've got nothing better to do. . . ."

"Come with me." Raj said. He led them into the wedding chapel and pointed to the first row of pews. "Wait here. The wedding will start in a few minutes." He eyed the four of them and settled on Toast. "You," he said, pointing to Toast. "Follow me."

"What? Why?" Toast asked.

"You'll see," Raj promised. He and Toast disappeared behind a blue sequined curtain.

Kylie, Jenn, and Sam settled into the front pew. "A real wedding!" Jenn gushed. "This is so exciting!"

A bride and a groom, both in their thirties, appeared at the back of the chapel. The bride wore a short white dress and the groom wore a gold sharkskin suit.

"This is going to be fun," Kylie whispered to Jenn.

A recording of the wedding march began to blare out of a speaker at the front of the church. The bride and groom walked down the short aisle and stopped at the altar. The sequined curtain moved and Raj and Toast jumped out—both dressed like Elvis!

Kylie laughed. "Look at Toast!" He wore a white jumpsuit with fringe, a shiny black Elvis wig with long sideburns, and tinted glasses. Raj was dressed exactly the same way.

Cheesy canned applause blasted out of the speaker. Raj bowed and said, "Thang you, thang you very much" in an Indian-accented Elvis voice. He pushed Toast toward the groom. "Here's your best man," he told the groom.

The bride reached over and pinched Toast's cheek. "I've heard of Young Elvis and Fat Elvis," she cooed. "You must be Cute Elvis."

"Ma'am," Toast drawled in his best Elvis accent. "Pinch me one more time and I might get 'all shook up.'"

Kylie cracked up at Toast's joke.

"Get up here, girls," Raj said to her and Jenn. "This bride needs some bridesmaids."

Kylie and Jenn joined the bride at the altar. "Today we bring together two very special people," Raj began. "People I've come to know and love. Charles—"

The groom interrupted him. "That's Carl."

"Right," Raj said. "Carl and Leanne."

"Diane," the bride corrected him.

"Carl and Diane," Raj said. "Welcome to Las Vegas. I now pronounce you man and wife."

Raj burst into an Elvis song. Carl and Diane clapped. Toast tossed some rice. "I love this!" Diane cried.

"Tips are graciously accepted," Raj reminded them. "And if your check bounces, you'll spend your *honeymoon singing 'Jailhouse Rock.'"*

"Viva Las Vegas!" Kylie called out.

"Miles and miles of oranges," Taylor said. She sat in the front seat of Charly's truck as they drove through an endless orange grove. The truck was ancient and rusty and it sputtered and coughed as it rambled down the dusty country road. Lyndi and Danny huddled in the flatbed at the back, wrapped in blankets. It was getting dark.

"You know a glass of orange juice has no fat, no cholesterol, no salt, and provides one hundred twenty percent of your daily vitamin C," Charly recited.

"You're an expert on oranges," Taylor observed.

"I work in these groves," Charly confessed. "After school and on weekends."

Taylor didn't know what to say. Charly's clothes were ragged and dirty, her truck was rickety and old, and she had to work picking oranges. She must be very poor, *Taylor thought.*

"It's great," Charly added, smiling. "I get to spend more time with my dad that way."

"Your dad picks oranges?" Taylor asked.

"Millions," Charly replied.

Poor Charly, *Taylor thought.*

"Do you have dances and proms at your school?" Charly asked.

Taylor nodded. "You don't?"

"No," Charly replied. "I'm home-schooled."

"Listen," Taylor began. "Let us pay you for the gas—and give you something extra for your trouble."

Charly shook her head. "No. I'm just glad for the company."

The engine jolted and started making weird chugging sounds. The truck slowed to a crawl, then stopped.

"What's wrong?" Taylor asked.

"No big deal," Charly explained. "Happens all the time."

She jumped out of the cab. Taylor followed. Lyndi and Danny hopped off the back.

"I think your truck has gone to that big scrap yard in the sky," Danny said.

Charly grabbed a toolbox from the back of the truck, then went around to the front and opened the hood. "Don't worry," she assured them. "We'll be fine."

It was getting dark quickly. "What else can go wrong?" Taylor wailed. She paced near the front of the truck, mumbling to herself. "People do it every day. Planes, cars, trains, buses. Los Angeles to Salt Lake City. It really happens. Not for us, but it really happens. . . ."

Charly popped her head out from under the hood. "You want to go to Salt Lake?" she asked.

"Yes," Taylor replied. "For the Olympics."

"Why didn't you say so? I thought you wanted to go to Las Vegas," Charly said.

"To catch a flight to Salt Lake," Taylor explained.

"Heck, my dad will take you straight to Salt Lake," Charly offered.

"No, thanks," Danny said, eyeing the broken-down truck. "I don't ride mules."

"We'll go on his plane," Charly said.

Taylor glanced at Lyndi and Danny. Lyndi shrugged. *Is Charly nuts? Taylor thought.*

"Sure," Danny joked. "Then he can take us to Hawaii on his yacht."

"Make up your mind," Charly said. "Do you want the plane or the yacht?"

"Charly, what are you talking about?" Kylie asked.

Charly pointed to some lights at the end of the orange grove. Kylie could just make out a huge mansion.

"That's my house," Charly told them. "My father owns these orange groves. And he has his own private jet!"

"What?" Kylie gasped. Then she started laughing. Charly wasn't poor at all. She was super-rich!

chapter eight

"Don't you love Las Vegas?" Ashley asked me. She and I were hanging in the lobby of our hotel after lunch one day. "The neon lights at night. Hot afternoons by the pool. Sometimes I can't believe how lucky we are. I mean, shooting a movie *and* going on location to Vegas? It's so cool!"

"I know," I agreed. "I'm really loving this."

She shifted on the couch. "We're leaving for Park City soon," she said. "There are a lot of interesting scenes in that part of the movie."

"What do you mean?" I asked.

"Well . . ." She looked uncomfortable and shifted again. "Like, for instance, your scene with Noah. The kissing scene."

"Oh, yeah." I wasn't exactly looking forward to that one.

"Are you nervous about it?" she asked.

"Kind of," I admitted. "It's going to be weird

kissing someone I don't like. Especially in front of a jillion people—and the camera."

"I wish *my* character could be the one who kisses him," she said.

I laughed. "Me, too." I paused. "You really like him, don't you?"

She nodded. "Don't you think he's talented?"

"I guess," I said. "I just don't think he's good enough for you."

Ashley stared at me. "Why not?"

Now it was my turn to feel uncomfortable. "I don't know. Don't you think he's a little . . . phony?"

"What?" she cried. "Why do you think he's phony?"

"Well, for one thing, did you know that he didn't get those blond streaks from all the time he spends on his board? He gets his hair highlighted."

"He does not," Ashley said.

"I heard Tom say so," I insisted.

"Tom the hairdresser? He was probably just teasing Noah."

"He wasn't," I said. "I could tell. And what about that first day on the set? You were talking to him and he interrupted you to chase after Don. Remember?"

"He's very focused on his acting career," Ashley said. "He's ambitious. There's nothing wrong with that."

I frowned. No matter what I said, Ashley just wouldn't see Noah as I did.

"Where's Christina today?" Ashley asked.

"She had some errands to run for Amy," I explained.

"I've been meaning to ask you," Ashley began. "Didn't you think it was weird when we stopped at that gas station a few days ago and she sat in that man's car?"

"Yeah," I admitted. "It did kind of surprise me. But Christina is very spontaneous. I like that about her."

Ashley raised an eyebrow. "Spontaneous? I'm not sure that's the word I would use. Maybe *irresponsible*. Or even *dangerous*."

"Dangerous?" I laughed. "Come on, Ashley. She's a little out there, maybe. But she's just trying to have fun."

Buddy bounded into the lobby. "Hey! Anybody up for a walk?" he asked. "I'm going to the Paradise Casino to see if I can score tickets for a concert."

"Who's playing?" I asked.

"Hard Drive," Buddy said. "One of my favorite bands. I tried to see them in L.A., but the tickets sold out in about two seconds."

"Jake loves Hard Drive," I said. "But I'm not really into them."

"Come with me anyway," Buddy suggested.

"Just to see the casino. I heard they have a volcano there that shoots out glitter lava!"

I jumped to my feet. "I'm in. What about you, Ashley?"

"I'm waiting for Delia and Rachel," she said.

"We can all go together," Buddy suggested. "I don't mind waiting a few minutes."

Ashley shook her head. "You guys go without us. We've got something we have to do."

I stared at her but she avoided my eyes. *What does she have to do?* I wondered. *And why is it such a big secret?*

"All right," I said. "Um, I guess I'll see you later."

"See you." Ashley waved to us as Buddy and I left the hotel.

"So, who's Jake?" Buddy asked when we hit the street. "You mentioned that he likes Hard Drive?"

"Oh." I smiled at the thought of Jake. "He's my boyfriend."

I hadn't mentioned it to anyone, but I really missed Jake. At first I thought having Christina around might help, but it didn't. Christina was nothing like Jake.

I looked up. Buddy was watching me. "Jake must be pretty cool," he said.

"He is. We started going out last spring," I explained. "But we weren't together very long when I went away for the summer. And then this movie came along. . . ."

"And you're away from him again," Buddy finished. "Hmmm . . ." He looked thoughtful.

"What?" I asked.

"Oh, nothing," he said.

"Buddy—you looked like you were about to say something," I prompted.

"Well . . ." He stopped dead in front of a supermarket. "No matter how much you miss Jake, just remember that he misses you ten times more. Though he'll never admit it."

"What? How do you know that?"

"It's the big secret of guys everywhere," he explained. "We always try to act cool in front of girls. But really we're as mushy as you are."

"Oh, Buddy," I scoffed. "That's not true."

Buddy grinned at me. "Well, I'll tell you what *is* true. If a guy has a girl like you or Ashley, he's lucky. And he knows it."

I smiled. "Thanks." We kept walking down the street. I felt a lot better—kind of warm inside. And it was all because of Buddy.

I shook my head. Buddy really was the nicest guy. If only Ashley could see him that way—she'd be crazy about him!

"I wonder what Ashley's up to," I said. "Why do you think she wouldn't tell us where she was going with Delia and Rachel?"

"Maybe it's me," Buddy said.

"You?" I asked. "What do you mean?"

"Maybe she was making up an excuse not to go with us—because she doesn't want to be with me," Buddy suggested. "I mean, I really, really like Ashley. But she's always hanging with Noah. And she barely looks at me. I don't know why."

"Buddy," I began, "you're a great guy. But maybe you could, I don't know . . . spruce yourself up a little."

He glanced down at his wrinkled T-shirt. "What do you mean?"

"Well," I began, "maybe if you cleaned up your table manners a little, and paid a little more attention to your clothes, and put some gel in your hair—that kind of thing. Then Ashley might notice you more."

"You think?" Buddy asked.

"If she got to know you better, I really think Ashley would like you," I told him. "And you're so funny! Ashley loves funny guys."

"Really?" Buddy said. "I saw her laughing when we shot that wedding scene. You know, where I play Elvis?"

I chuckled at the memory of it. "Yeah, that was hilarious. Your Elvis imitation is really good."

"Hey," Buddy said. "I wonder if that would work. . . ."

"What?" I asked.

"What if I wore my Elvis costume—and sang to Ashley? Serenaded her outside her room?"

"She'll love it!" I cried. "It'll be funny and romantic at the same time—just like you."

Buddy grinned. "It *is* kind of a funny idea, isn't it?"

"I'll ask Christina to borrow the costume from wardrobe tomorrow," I offered. "And you can serenade Ashley tomorrow night! It's our last night in Vegas before we move on to Park City—the perfect time for a sentimental song from Elvis."

I clapped my hand on his shoulder. "Buddy," I said, "after tomorrow night Ashley will never look at you the same way again."

"What do you think?" I asked Rachel and Delia. I turned in front of the mirror in my hotel room. I was wearing a white Elvis outfit covered with fringe and sequins and metal studs.

"You look amazing, Ashley," Delia told me.

"Very cute," Rachel agreed.

I was able to sneak the costume out of wardrobe right after Mary-Kate's scene yesterday. I had to admit, it looked pretty good on me. "I just hope Noah will think so," I said.

"Ashley, trust me," Rachel said. "After tomorrow night, Noah will never look at you the same way again."

● ● ●

"Hey, Mary-Kate," Delia called to me the next night. "We're all going out to eat. Want to come?"

The elevator door had just opened onto our floor of the hotel. Christina and I stepped off to find Delia, Ashley, Rachel, Buddy, Noah, and Kip on their way out.

I hadn't spent time with the other cast members in a while, and I thought it sounded like fun. But before I could say yes, Christina answered for me.

"No, thanks," she said. "We've got other plans."

Ashley shrugged, but I could see in her eyes that she was a little hurt. "Okay," she said. "We'll see you later." They boarded the elevator and the doors slid shut.

"What other plans?" I asked Christina. "We didn't make any plans. Why can't we go out with the others?"

"I was hoping we could talk," Christina said to me. "Let's go out to dinner on our own."

We went back to our room and changed. Then we wandered down the strip until we came to an Italian café. Christina stopped to study the menu.

"Look—panini!" she exclaimed. "They're grilled Italian sandwiches. I used to have one for lunch every Saturday in New York."

"Why don't we eat here then?" I suggested. We went inside. The restaurant was crowded. We took the last free table, near the door.

"It must be fun to live in New York," I said after

we'd ordered sandwiches and coffee. "What part of the city did you live in?"

"Greenwich Village." Christina sighed. "It *is* fun living there. The streets are full of people all the time, day and night. You can walk everywhere, so you never have to drive. I don't have my license yet. I guess I'll need it now that I'll be living in L.A."

"I just got my license a few months ago," I told her. "Don't worry—the test isn't that hard. Of course I failed on my first try!"

Christina laughed. "You did? And you're such a good driver. I don't have a prayer!"

"You'll be fine," I assured her. "Just don't have Jake around to distract you!"

"Hey, don't worry," Christina said. "Jake's my cousin. I like him a lot, but I don't find him distracting."

The waiter brought our sandwiches. "Did Jake's family ever visit you in New York?" I asked Christina.

"Sure," she replied. "One year Jake and his parents came for Christmas. That was a long time ago, before his brother and sister were born. He must have been about nine, maybe, and I was eight."

"What was he like then?" I asked. "I can't imagine him as a little kid."

"He was really sweet and fun," Christina told me. "A lot like he is now, actually. We had such a great time together that Christmas. We went ice-skating in Central Park and shopping at the big toy stores. My dad even took us for a carriage ride." She put down her sandwich. "We used to be very close when we were little."

She looked sad, I thought. "What happened?"

"We're still close in a way," she said. "But we haven't seen each other in four or five years. My parents used to bring me out to visit every summer, but the last few years—" She paused to nibble on her sandwich. "There have been some problems. And people change a lot from age eleven to age sixteen. I'm not the same little kid Jake used to know."

"But you said he's basically the same," I reminded her. "Maybe you are, too."

She shook her head. "Jake will never change. He's a little sensitive—his feelings get hurt easily. But he's solid. He likes to do the right thing. He was born that way. He'll always be that way."

I was glad to hear her describe the Jake I knew and loved. "And what about you?"

"I'm always changing," she said. "My mother says I go through a new phase every six months. It drives her crazy. She never knows who I'll be next!"

We finished our sandwiches and coffee. I was in the mood for something sweet. "Want to get some frozen yogurt?" I suggested. "There's an ice cream place down the street. Why don't we pay our check and walk down there?"

"You go ahead," Christina said. "I'll settle the check and meet you there."

I reached for my wallet. "No, we'll split the check. Why should you pay?"

"Please—let me treat you," Christina insisted. "I want to. You brought me along on this trip and let me hang around your movie set. It's been great. This is the least I can do after all you've done for me."

"Thanks, Christina. That's so nice of you."

"I don't want any ice cream or anything," she said. "You go ahead. I'll meet you there in a few minutes."

"Okay." I left the restaurant and walked down the street to the ice cream shop. I ordered a strawberry yogurt and sat at a counter to wait for Christina. A few minutes later she ran into the shop, breathless and laughing.

"Christina—what happened?" I asked.

"You won't believe it." She paused to catch her breath. Then she ran to the door, cracked it open, and peered down the street.

"What's going on?" I asked again.

She ducked back inside. "They're not following me. I'm safe!"

"Safe?" I asked. "What are you talking about? And who would be following you?"

"The waiter from the restaurant," Christina said. "I skipped out on the check!"

chapter nine

The blood drained from my face. I couldn't believe I heard her right. "You what?"

"I skipped out on the check," Christina repeated. "It wasn't much—we only had sandwiches."

"How could you do that?" I demanded. "I would have paid for it if you didn't have the money!"

"That's not the point," Christina insisted. "That place was way overpriced. And they're owned by a big corporation—their parent company exploits poor people in foreign countries! We did a good thing by not giving them our money!"

"If they're so terrible we shouldn't have eaten there in the first place," I countered. "And, anyway, what about the waiter? He lost his tip—and he might have to cover the cost of our meal! Christina, how could you do that? It's stealing!"

"I live by my own rules." She sniffed.

"That doesn't make it right," I said.

She began to look less sure of herself. "I've never done it before, I swear," she said. "I won't do it again. I just wanted to see what it felt like."

I was starting to wonder about Christina. I couldn't imagine running out of a restaurant without paying. How could I be friends with someone who would do something like that?

"Listen Christina," I said. "I like you. But I can't hang out with you if you keep doing stuff like this."

"I'm sorry, Mary-Kate," Christina said. She sat down at the counter next to me. "You're right. That was a stupid thing to do. I just . . . lately I feel like everything's turned upside down. The only time I really feel happy is when I'm doing something exciting, you know?"

"There are lots of exciting things you can do that aren't illegal," I pointed out.

"You don't understand," she said. "My parents are splitting up—that's why Mom and I are moving to L.A."

I froze, momentarily stunned. Whoa. Christina's parents were getting divorced? Why hadn't Jake told me about that?

"The last few years have been horrible," Christina went on. "Mom is so upset she can hardly get out of bed. My mom sent me to Jake's family to get me out of her way! And my dad has a new girlfriend who doesn't want me around, either."

Christina paused. I watched as she blinked back tears.

"I don't have any friends here," she said. "You're so lucky. You'll always have your sister, Ashley. But I can't count on anyone—not even my parents!"

A huge lump formed in my throat. I felt terrible for Christina. I thought of how much I depended on family—what would I do if I had no one?

"You've been so nice to me," Christina continued. "Since I met you, I finally feel like I have someone I can count on—you know?"

She snatched a napkin from a dispenser on the counter and wiped her eyes. "It's so embarrassing—crying in an ice cream shop like this."

Now I understood why Christina acted so weird. She was upset. She needed someone she could count on. She was crying out for help.

"Come on," I said, tossing my yogurt container into the trash. "Let's go back to the restaurant and pay the check."

We were quiet on the walk back. I kept running through what she'd told me. I really liked Christina—and I felt sorry for her.

Some of the things she does are not cool, I told myself, *but she's just going through a hard time. She needs sympathy and understanding.*

By the time we walked into the restaurant, I

knew what I had to do. I was going to stick by Christina. I was going to help her by being her friend.

"That's funny," Mary-Kate said, riffling through her wallet. "I'm missing a ten-dollar bill."

We'd just finished our last day of filming in Las Vegas. Mary-Kate, Christina, and I were walking back to the hotel that afternoon. Mary-Kate wanted to stop and buy a T-shirt she spotted in a shop on the way.

"I know I had a ten and a twenty in here," Mary-Kate insisted. She held up the twenty. No sign of the ten.

"Are you sure?" I asked her, peeking into her wallet.

"Totally sure." Mary-Kate frowned. "Could I have dropped it somewhere?"

"Oh, hey," Christina interjected. "I almost forgot. I took ten dollars out of your wallet this morning."

I glared at Christina. How could she just help herself to Mary-Kate's money like that?

"You did?" Mary-Kate said. "Why?"

"I didn't have time to go the cash machine," Christina explained. "I was going to pay you back tonight after I hit an ATM. Sorry, I should have said something."

"No problem," Mary-Kate said. "Just pay me back when you get the chance."

I turned my gaze to Mary-Kate. Why was she

being so cool about this? Christina was practically stealing from her!

We walked into the shop. Christina wandered toward the back and tried on some hats. I pulled Mary-Kate aside.

"How can you let her get away with that?" I whispered.

"It's fine," Mary-Kate said. "She's going to pay me back."

"But don't you think it's weird that she'd just go through your wallet and take money without asking you?" I insisted. "What if you hadn't noticed the money was missing? Would she have mentioned that she borrowed it from you at all?"

"Look," Mary-Kate said, "don't worry about Christina. She's going through a weird situation right now. You don't understand."

I think I do understand, I thought, frowning. *And I don't like it. Not one bit.*

"All right, Ashley," I coached myself that night. "This is it. Are you really going to go through with it?"

I stood in front of the mirror in my room, wearing the white Elvis jumpsuit, staring at my reflection one last time. The costume sparkled in the light.

Noah will definitely know how I feel about him once I serenade him in this thing, I thought. *But will he say he feels the same way about me?*

I'd sent Rachel and Delia down to the lobby. I wanted to do this on my own. If it's a disaster, I figured, the fewer witnesses the better.

I opened my door and peeked into the hall. It was empty. Perfect. And I was pretty sure Noah was in his room. I'd seen him go in there after dinner.

I took a deep breath. *All right,* I thought. *Here goes nothing.*

The jumpsuit jangled as I walked down the hall. I knocked on Noah's door. The door opened. There stood Noah, with Kip hovering behind him.

Just go for it! I told myself.

"Noah Atkins," I drawled in my best Elvis voice. "You have an Elvis-gram." Then I started singing "Love Me Tender."

While I sang, I watched Noah's face. He was smiling. *That's got to be a good sign,* I thought.

Down the hall a door opened. A man popped his head out of the room to see what was going on. Then the elevator dinged, and Rachel and Delia came out. They tried to hide at the end of the hall, but I spotted them.

Those sneaks! I thought. I knew they'd try to catch this somehow.

I glanced at Noah's face again. He was still grinning.

Then I heard a strange sound. Another voice— singing the same song! I turned my head toward the sound, which was coming from down the hall.

I couldn't believe it! Standing at the other end of the hall was—another Elvis!

Still singing, I stared at the other Elvis. He was tall and skinny, with messy brown hair and the tail of his shirt hanging out of his pants. . . . Buddy!

He ran down the hall and fell onto his knees in front of me, still singing!

My jaw dropped. Noah stepped into the hallway to see what was going on.

He took one look at Buddy, there on his knees, dressed up as Elvis, and burst out laughing.

"Dude—Elvises are taking over the building!" Kip cried out.

Everybody started laughing. In the back of my mind, I knew it had to be a funny sight, one Elvis singing to another. But I was mortified. Buddy ruined everything—and now I felt like an idiot.

I brushed past Buddy and ran to my room, slamming the door behind me. I threw myself on my bed and covered my head with my pillows.

Someone knocked on the door. "Ashley! Ashley, open up. It's me—Buddy!"

I could still hear everyone laughing in the hall. There was no way I was opening that door.

"Ashley, what's wrong?" Buddy called.

"Go away, Buddy!" I shouted. "Go away and leave me alone!"

chapter ten

"What's going on?" I asked. Christina and I got off the elevator to see a small crowd gathered in the hallway, laughing. Then a small blond blur dressed in white flashed by.

Ashley! She ran into her room and slammed the door in Buddy's face!

"Man, you missed it, Mary-Kate!" Kip said. "There were two Elvises and they were both singing the same song. It was freaky!"

I glanced at Noah, who was laughing as hard as anyone.

Oh, no, I thought. *Two Elvises? Something was wrong here. Very wrong.*

I hurried over to Buddy, who stood outside Ashley's room, begging her to open the door.

"Come on, Buddy," I said, leading him away toward my room. "If she's upset, she won't come out for hours."

"What happened?" Christina asked him.

He slumped into a chair. "It's the weirdest thing," he explained. "Somehow, Ashley had the same idea we had! She was dressed up as Elvis—only she was singing to Noah."

Christina let a short giggle escape, then stifled it. *Poor Buddy,* I thought. His big brown eyes looked sadder than ever. *He really likes Ashley. And now it looks like he doesn't have a chance with her.*

"Ashley told me to leave her alone. She never wants to see me again," he said. "I guess our plan backfired."

"She doesn't mean it, Buddy," I told him. "She's just upset right now. And anyway, she *has* to see you again. We all have to work together for another week!"

Buddy drooped. "Yeah—she'll have to see me on the set. But that doesn't count."

It was awful to see Buddy look so sad. I glanced at Christina, who shook her head. I couldn't believe Ashley would be so hard on him! He was only trying to be nice to her!

"It's not right. All Ashley is thinking about is Noah!" Christina said.

Christina was right. But this just wasn't like Ashley.

Ashley tried hard not to hurt other people—I knew that. So why did she have to hurt Buddy's feelings this way? What had gotten into her?

"Tomorrow we're going to shoot in Park City," I said, trying to cheer Buddy up. "No more Vegas. No more Elvis. Everything will be different there. Ashley will get over this fast—you'll see."

Buddy nodded, but I didn't think he believed me. I wasn't so sure I believed myself.

"Look!" Jenn cried. "There's Taylor!"

Kylie gasped. The door of the beautiful private jet slid open. There stood Taylor with a stylishly dressed girl with long brown hair. That must be Charly, Kylie thought.

Taylor waved to them. Kylie, Jenn, Toast, and Sam hurried across the tarmac and boarded the plane.

Kylie hugged Taylor. "Nice ride, sister," she said.

"You can have only so much bad luck," Taylor declared. "At some point it's going to change."

Kylie gazed at the plush interior of the plane. "This is change, all right," she said.

"Everyone—this is Charly Simms," Taylor announced.

"I want to thank you all for inviting me along," Charly said.

"You're thanking us?" Kylie cried. "Charly, you're our guardian angel!"

"You're delivering us to the snow," Sam said.

"You're our snow angel," Taylor put in.

"So, your dad is the orange king of California, huh?" Toast asked. "You didn't happen to bring any oranges with you, did you?"

Charly laughed. "You must be Roast. I've heard all about you. And I'll bet you're hungry."

"That's Toast," Toast corrected her. "And how did you know?"

The jet's engine began to roar. "Everyone, sit down and buckle your seat belts," Charly said. "We're off to Utah!"

"To Park City!" Taylor cheered. "And the Olympics!"

"I love this place!" Danny exclaimed. Taylor, Kylie, and their friends wandered down a snowy street in Park City, searching for a good place to watch the Olympics on TV. Alex Reisher was skiing in the downhill that afternoon and Taylor didn't want to miss it. She'd tried to get tickets to see him live, but they were all sold out—of course.

Danny slid on the icy sidewalk. "Look—you can skate on the street here! Toast, do a run-and-slide."

Taylor glanced at Toast. She remembered the conversation she'd overheard between Toast and Jenn, about how Danny made jokes at Toast's expense. This looked like another one of those times.

Toast said, "Run-and-slide. All right." But he looked nervous.

Don't do it, *Taylor thought.* You know you'll just

look silly—or maybe even get hurt.

Toast prepared to run and slide on the ice. But Jenn said, "Toast—hey."

Taylor caught a secret glance between them. Toast straightened up and said, "No, Danny—you do it."

Danny looked surprised. "Me? But you're the Toast-man!"

"I'll fall on my butt and make a fool of myself," Toast said. "I won't do it."

Way to go, Toast, *Taylor* thought. Don't let Danny push you around.

"You got me wrong," Danny protested. "I'm not setting you up to fall on your butt—I swear."

"Okay," Toast said. "Then you slide."

"Fine," Danny agreed. He took a running start down the street, then suddenly changed his mind and stopped. But he slipped on the ice anyway and fell on his butt.

Everyone laughed—except for Lyndi. "Poor Danny!" she cried, running over to help him. "Are you hurt?"

Danny struggled to his feet but didn't say a word. His face was bright red.

"Good going, Toast," Jenn said.

Taylor nodded and smiled at him. Toast was starting to change, she noticed. He was getting more—what was the word—dignified? No, that wasn't quite right. More sure of himself, maybe.

"How about this place, Taylor?" Kylie asked. She

stopped in front of a coffeehouse. "They've got two big-screen TVs."

Sam nodded his approval. "This looks like a Sam hang."

They went inside, settled at a table, and watched the race. "Alex Reisher is up!" Taylor cried out. Her heart raced at the sight of the skier.

"Come on, Alex," she murmured as he leaned into the starting gate. Then he was off.

"Go, Alex!" Taylor cheered. "Go, Alex!"

Soon the whole coffeehouse was chanting "Go, Alex! Go, Alex!"

"He's on world-record pace!" Taylor shouted. "One last turn and he's got the gold!"

Her heart pounded as she watched him take the last turn—and tumble into the deep snow!

"Oh, no!" Everyone groaned.

Alex pulled himself to his feet, unhurt. But his chances for a medal were ruined.

Taylor tried to hide her disappointment. "There's always two thousand six in Turin."

Charly patted Taylor's hand. "Sorry, Taylor."

"He'll be back," Taylor said. "He's only twenty."

"I'm seventeen," Sam interrupted. "And I'll be snowboarding after lunch."

"Excellent. I'm ready," Toast said.

"Any of you girls interested?" Sam asked, eyeing Kylie.

Kylie, Taylor, Jenn, and Charly all shook their heads. "We're going skiing," Kylie explained.

But Lyndi piped up, "Ummm—are you going snowboarding, Danny?"

Danny nodded.

"I love snowboarding!" Lyndi squealed. "I'll join you."

Sam looked doubtful. "You can bust huge air?" he asked her. "You won't be cratering into a bank?"

"Huh?" Lyndi asked. Then, faking it, she added, "I snow-go with my board-o."

Taylor rolled her eyes. Lyndi didn't know anything about snowboarding. "I'll go with you, Lynd," she offered.

"Cool!" Toast cried. "'Cause I am stomped to stoke and stick."

"Uh—yeah," Lyndi said. "Me, too. I'm stomped."

Sam and Toast cruised down the mountain on their snowboards. "Come on, Lyndi, let's go," Taylor said. But Lyndi stood on her snowboard, rooted to the spot. She clung to Taylor's arm, terrified.

Danny boarded up to her. "Lyndi, the idea is to slide down the hill on the cold white stuff."

"I know, I know." Lyndi's face was white. She took a deep breath and pushed herself away from Taylor. She slid about five feet down the hill.

"I'm doing it!" she squealed.

Crash! *She went down. But she quickly sat up, smiling.*

"You've never done this before, have you, Lyndi?" Danny asked.

"No," Lyndi admitted. "I just thought it would be fun to try it with you."

Taylor checked out Danny's reaction. He'd always avoided Lyndi before. But this time he smiled at her.

"All right." He reached for her arm and helped her up. "Let's give it a try."

They tried to board together. Danny propped Lyndi up. They managed to go about ten feet before they crashed into the snow together, laughing.

She's starting to grow on him, *Taylor thought.* This is my cue to leave them alone.

Kylie licked the last bit of marshmallow off her lips and took a sip of hot chocolate. "Ah." She sighed. "This is my favorite part of skiing."

She sat snuggled by the fire in the lodge that evening. Taylor and Charly were making s'mores. Lyndi rubbed a sore spot on Danny's neck. Toast and Jenn sipped hot cider together on the love seat. And Sam hovered near Kylie. It was the only thing bothering her on an otherwise perfect evening—Sam was sticking to her like glue.

Jenn got to her feet. "I'm going to call it a night. You coming, Lyndi?"

101

"I'm staying to work on Danny's snowboard injury," Lyndi answered.

"Snowboard injury," Toast snorted. "That's rich."

Danny stood up. "That's all right, Lyndi. I'll walk you back to your room." He reached for her hand, helped her up—and didn't let go.

Kylie shot a glance at Taylor. Did she see that? Taylor nodded at her as if she'd known about it all along.

The others got up to go, too. Sam said, "Hey, Kylie, stick around. We'll have a hot chocolate nightcap."

Kylie caught Jenn and Taylor watching her. "Um—okay. Sure," she replied. She could feel Taylor's eyes burning into her. She knew what Taylor was thinking. Why would Kylie want to be alone with Sam? But Kylie knew it was time to set things straight once and for all.

The others left. Sam waited until he was sure they were gone. Then he moved closer to Kylie.

"What are you doing?" Kylie asked.

Sam didn't answer. He just leaned forward and kissed her.

Kylie pushed him away. "Sam—chill," she said.

Sam shrugged and acted innocent. "What?"

"Do you see the problem here?" Kylie demanded. "In your head we should be boyfriend and girlfriend. But what about what's in my head and my heart?"

"You're not into it?" Sam asked. Kylie couldn't believe he hadn't gotten the message yet.

"No, I'm not," she told him. "Charcoal has become black and white."

"Kylie, I know you like me," Sam insisted.

How dense can a guy be? Kylie wondered. "Liking and kissing are two different things," she explained. "Sam, it takes two people to kiss. Two people who both want to kiss. I'm not into it, so, sorry."

She stood up and walked away. For once Sam didn't follow her.

At the door she glanced back at him. He sat on the couch, staring at the ceiling.

Finally, she thought. He's finally gotten the message.

"Mary-Kate is great in this scene," Rachel whispered to me.

I nodded. We were on the set in Park City, and Mary-Kate and Noah were shooting the scene where their characters, Kylie and Sam, are supposed to kiss. Rachel and I stood on the side, watching. Why couldn't I be the one who gets to kiss Noah? I thought. It was weird watching the boy I liked try to kiss my sister!

Mary-Kate pushed Noah away and the scene ended. Everyone applauded. Mary-Kate really was very convincing. It was almost as if she weren't acting at all.

Beaming, Mary-Kate stepped off the set and approached me and Rachel. "How was it?" she asked.

"Very believable," Rachel told her.

"Totally," I agreed. "No one would ever guess that you and Noah are best friends in real life."

Mary-Kate smirked at my joke. "Very funny. It was so weird, though—kissing a guy in a movie. Totally freaky."

"Mary-Kate!" Christina called from the wardrobe room. "Can I see you a minute? Amy and I want you to try on a few things for your ski scenes."

"Wait until you see the ski outfits," I told Mary-Kate. "They're so slick."

"Awesome," Mary-Kate said. "See you guys later." She hurried over toward the wardrobe room.

"I'm going to hit the hot tub before dinner," Rachel said. "Want to come?"

I spied Noah across the room. He'd been talking to Don but now he was headed my way. I didn't want to see him. I'd been avoiding him ever since the Elvis-gram disaster. I was too embarrassed to talk to him.

"Hot tub sounds good," I said to Rachel. "Let's get out of here."

We turned to leave, but Noah called out, "Ashley—wait!"

I stopped. Noah ran toward us.

Rachel grinned at me. "You're on your own. See you later." She left the set.

My pulse raced. *What does he want?* I wondered nervously. *To laugh at me some more?*

"Ashley—listen," Noah said. "I want to apologize to you for that last night in Vegas. You looked cool in your Elvis costume—and you're an excellent singer."

"But—you were laughing your head off," I reminded him.

"I know—I'm sorry. I didn't mean to laugh at you. But when I saw Buddy. . . the two Elvises . . . it was just so funny. I couldn't help it."

"Oh." Some apology this turned out to be. I started to walk away.

"Ashley, wait!" Noah touched my shoulder. "You don't get it. Funny is good! I like funny."

"You do?"

He nodded. "And I like you, too." He paused. "Do you want to have dinner with me tonight? Just you and me, none of the other kids."

I couldn't believe it. Noah was asking me out on a date—a real date. Finally!

"I'd love to," I replied.

Inside I felt like jumping up and down. A date with Noah! In a weird, inside-out way, my Elvis plan worked after all!

chapter eleven

"**I**'m afraid to talk to her, Mary-Kate," Buddy confided to me. "I'm afraid to even look at her."

Buddy and I sat on the sundeck at the Stein Eriksen ski resort catching the last few rays of the afternoon. Part of the movie was set at the lodge, which wasn't far from Park City, so the cast and crew were staying there.

Buddy was so hung up on Ashley. I tried to comfort him. "You shouldn't be afraid of Ashley," I told him. "She's a reasonable person. You can talk to her."

Buddy shook his head. "What good would it do? She doesn't like me, anyway. Everybody knows she likes Noah."

I frowned. I couldn't believe that Ashley would prefer a puffhead like Noah to a solid guy like Buddy. She was focusing so much on Noah that she hadn't really gotten to know Buddy. I was sure she'd see the light—and I wasn't going to let Buddy give up.

"Ashley's no dummy," I told Buddy. "It won't be long before she sees Noah's for what he really is and loses interest in him."

"Do you really think so?" Buddy asked.

"Definitely," I promised. "You should talk to her. Tell her you didn't mean to embarrass her. She'll understand."

"All right I will," Buddy vowed. "I'll talk to her before dinner tonight. Maybe if it goes well we can even go and get something to eat afterward."

"Good idea," I said. "But, Buddy—listen. If you do go out for dinner with Ashley, remember—one mouthful at a time."

Buddy grinned. "Got it."

"Look at me!" I wailed. "This mountain air is so dry. It's making my skin all flaky!"

"Let me see, Ashley." Rachel studied my face. "I don't see anything," she declared. "But if your skin feels dry, put this cream on it."

I stood before her in my bathrobe, a towel wrapped around my wet hair. Rachel smeared green cream all over my face. "Leave it on for fifteen minutes," she instructed. "When you wipe it off, your skin will be moist and dewy."

"Thanks, Rachel." I was getting ready for my date with Noah that night and running late. I didn't really have fifteen minutes to spare for face cream. But if it would make me feel better it was worth it.

Someone knocked at the door. "Oh, no!" I whispered. "That can't be Noah already!"

There was no way I was opening the door. I couldn't let anyone see me like this! I went to the door and stared through the peephole.

It was Buddy! What did he want?

"Ashley!" Buddy shouted. "Are you there? Please open the door. I need to talk to you."

"Does that guy have the worst timing or what?" Rachel whispered to me.

I had to admit, I was annoyed. I didn't have time to talk to Buddy just then—and I didn't want him or anyone to see me in a bathrobe with green cream all over my face.

"Buddy—I don't have time to talk right now," I called through the door. "Maybe tomorrow, okay?"

"Ashley, you'd better hurry up and get ready," Rachel said. "Noah's going to be here any minute."

"Okay." I hurried into the bathroom to wipe the cream off my face. Buddy pounded on the door again.

"Please, Ashley!" he shouted. "It will only take a minute!"

"Rachel!" I called from the bathroom. "I can't talk to him now! What should I do?"

"Let me handle it," Rachel said. She shouted

through the door. "Can't you take a hint, Buddy? Ashley's busy right now. Leave her alone!"

"I can't believe it," I said to Buddy. He was sitting in my room, telling me about how Ashley wouldn't even open the door for him. "It's not like Ashley to be rude that way."

"I didn't think so, either," Buddy said. "But then Rachel told me to leave her alone!" He sighed and shook his head. "I just have to face the facts. Ashley hates me."

"Buddy—that's crazy," I said. "Ashley doesn't hate you—I'm sure she doesn't. There must be some misunderstanding . . ."

Christina burst into the room. "Hey, Buddy," she said. "How's life?"

"Lousy." Buddy stood up and went to the door. "I think I'll go to my room and order a pizza—or two or three." He left, closing the door behind him.

"What's with him?" Christina asked. "Is he still hung up on Ashley?"

"Yeah," I answered. "She's not being very nice to him. It worries me."

"Well, I've got something that will take your mind off it," Christina said. "While you were busy filming this afternoon, I went skiing."

"How's the powder?" I asked.

"Excellent!" Christina said. "I'm used to the icy

crud we ski on back east. The Rockies rule! And the guys aren't bad, either."

I laughed.

"I met a really cute guy on the slopes," Christina continued. "His name is Rob. He and his friend Justin want to meet us later. You up for it?"

I shrugged. "Sure, I guess so."

"Great. I'll call Rob and tell him we'll meet them around nine."

After an early dinner, I spent a couple of hours in my room, studying my lines. Christina sat on her bed, reading. At eight-thirty, she stood up and started putting on her ski outfit.

"What are you doing?" I asked. "I thought we were going out tonight."

"We are," she said. "You'd better change or we'll be late." She pulled my ski suit out of my closet and tossed it on my bed. "Don't forget your long underwear. It's cold out there tonight."

"What are you talking about?" I asked. "I thought we were meeting your friends Rob and Justin."

"Right," Christina said. "We're meeting them at nine—at the foot of the slopes. Did I forget to mention that?"

I still didn't get it. "But the slopes are closed for the night. We can't go skiing now. . . ."

"That's what makes it so cool!" Christina said. "Skiing at night! We'll have the slopes to ourselves! Rob and Justin can ride us up to the top in their snowmobiles—and we can ski under the stars. It will be great!"

"But—we can't do that!" I protested. "It's not allowed!"

"Not allowed?" Christina scoffed. "Come on, Mary-Kate—live a little! Can you imagine how gorgeous it will be out on the slopes at night? You'll never have another chance to do it. You'll remember this night as one of the best of your life."

"I'm sure it would be beautiful, but I don't feel right about it," I insisted.

"Look—we have to go," Christina said. "Rob and Justin are probably there already, waiting for us. We can't stand them up!"

I reluctantly got to my feet. "All right," I agreed. "We'll go meet them—but just so they won't be waiting for us all night." *Then we'll tell them we don't want to go up the slope,* I decided.

I dressed quickly and we hurried out to the ski slope. In the moonlight I could make out two guys standing near two snowmobiles loaded with skis.

"Hey! You made it!" A tall guy, about eighteen or nineteen waved us over. Strands of straight black hair stuck out from under his knit cap. "Christina, this is Justin."

111

The other guy, a little younger, with tight blond curls, said hello.

"Rob and Justin, this is my friend Mary-Kate," Christina said.

"Hey, Mary-Kate." Rob flashed his white teeth at me. "All right, girls, let's go!" He jumped onto his snowmobile and started it up. Christina jumped on the back. Justin motioned to me to get on his snowmobile, but I held back.

"Mary-Kate," Christina urged. "Come on!"

"Quick—before someone sees us!" Rob shouted over the roar of the engine.

I couldn't let Christina go by herself. What if something happened to her? Jake would never forgive me.

I had to go.

Justin helped me onto his snowmobile and we zoomed up the mountain.

How did I get myself into this? I thought.

chapter twelve

"I've wanted to be a movie star since I was six," Noah said. "Before that, I wanted to be a fireman."

"Really?" I watched the firelight flicker in Noah's blue eyes. I couldn't believe I was out on a date with him—and it was perfect. We were sharing a pot of fondue near a roaring fire in a cozy Swiss restaurant.

"Yeah." Noah stabbed a bit of bread with his fondue fork. "My mom says I was always a ham."

"I'll bet you were cute," I said.

"You should see my baby pictures." He dipped the bread in the melted cheese and twirled his fork.

"My dad keeps baby pictures of me and Mary-Kate in his wallet," I said. "He shows them to everybody! It's so embarrassing."

"I'll bet." Noah popped the cheesy bread into his mouth. "So, what do you think? You've seen my acting. Do you think I've got what it takes?"

I hesitated. Noah was as good-looking as any

movie star. And he was good in the movie we were shooting. But his character—Sam—was not exactly a stretch for him. Noah and Sam were a lot alike.

"Anything's possible," I said. "But I can't predict the future."

"Sure you can," Noah said. "Go ahead."

I laughed and playfully grabbed his hand, pretending to read his palm. "All right," I agreed. "I see great things for you." I traced my finger along a crease in his palm. "I see super-stardom!"

"Super-stardom! Yes!" Noah took my hand and pulled it toward his lips. "I hope your prediction comes true." He pressed his lips to my hand, then let it drop.

My hand throbbed where he'd kissed it. *Maybe now he'll start to talk about us,* I thought. *Instead of just himself.*

But he didn't. "I can't wait to get back to L.A.," he said. "I've got a couple of auditions lined up."

"Maybe we'll see each other in L.A.," I suggested.

"Yeah," he said. "Wouldn't it be cool if we both got the same agent?"

I sighed. I didn't want to admit it to myself, but in the back of my mind I knew it was true. Noah was kind of dull. All this talk about show business—it was all he could think about! He wasn't interested in anything—or anyone—else.

I helped myself to some fondue. I watched Noah

while I ate. The firelight made the blond streaks in his hair gleam. "Isn't this fondue good?" I asked.

"Mmm-hmm." He flashed me his trademark smile. I melted.

He may be a little dull, I thought. *But he's so cute!*

"Wow." I gasped. I perched at the top of the ski slope and gazed at the sky. The full moon glowed on the pearly snow. It was so bright you could see the trails clearly.

"Isn't it beautiful?" Christina asked. "Aren't you glad you came?"

"Come on, girls," Rob said. "Let's carve a groove into this mountain!"

I guess I have no choice, I thought, staring down the slope. *I'm here now—I might as well enjoy it!*

Rob, Christina, and I shussed down the slope. Justin drove one of the snowmobiles and met us at the bottom.

"Woo-hoo!" Rob whooped. "Now that's skiing! Nobody in our way—nothing but moonlight and snow!"

"It is beautiful," I admitted. "That was really fun. So—we did it. Let's go back to the lodge now."

"No way," Justin said. "It's my turn to ski."

Rob took Justin's place on the snowmobile. Christina and Justin piled on.

"Get on, Mary-Kate!" Christina shouted. "We're going again!"

I shook my head.

"You have to come with us!" Rob told me. "There's no other way for you to get back to the lodge!"

I realized I'd be stuck on the mountain if I didn't go with them. I got on the back of the snowmobile and we zipped up the mountain .

"All right!" Christina shouted as we skied down the slope again. "This is the best!"

But as we got near the bottom, I saw red lights flashing on the snow.

"What's that?" I asked.

We skied into a clearing at the foot of the hill. Someone was waiting for us there. The ski patrol!

"Remove your skis and come with us," a patrolman said over a loudspeaker. "You're all under arrest."

chapter thirteen

"**I** can't believe you girls would do something so dangerous." Don Maneri, our director, paced the waiting room of ski patrol headquarters.

"We're so sorry, Don," I said. "You're right—it was totally stupid."

"Who were those boys you were with?" Don demanded. "Did you even know them?"

I glanced at Christina. "I met Rob today," she admitted. "He seemed like a cool guy—"

"The ski patrol told me he used to be an instructor at the resort," Don interrupted. "He was fired last week for reckless behavior. He 'borrowed' those snowmobiles you were riding. That's how he put it, anyway. I'd call it stealing."

I shut my eyes and dropped my head into my hands. This was getting worse and worse.

The captain of the ski patrol walked into the room. "Justin Berg," he called.

Justin, who was sitting across the room with his mother, jumped to his feet. "Yes, sir," he replied.

"You're free to go," the captain told him. "Mary-Kate and Christina—"

We looked up at the captain. "You can go, too," he told us. "Mr. Maneri will take you back to your room."

"Thank you, Captain," Don said. "Let's go, girls."

We returned to the resort in silence. I felt so bad about letting Don down.

I should never have let myself get talked into doing such a stupid thing! I told myself. *The next time Christina tries to tempt me into doing something wild, I'm going to put my foot down.*

Don walked us back to our room. "Good night, girls. Get some sleep, and I'll see you in the morning."

"Thanks, Don," I said as he walked back to his room.

"I can't believe he didn't punish us!" Christina whispered to me as I opened the door to our room.

"Maybe he thought being picked up by the ski patrol was punishment enough," I grumbled. "It sure was enough for me."

"Mary-Kate, I heard what happened." I turned and found Ashley sitting on my bed. She didn't look happy. "Are you all right?" she asked.

"Yes," I told her. "We're fine."

"I can't believe that you would do something so

totally stupid!" Ashley said.

"I think I'll go downstairs and get something to drink," Christina said, slipping out of the room.

Ashley waited until Christina was gone. I'd never seen her so mad at me. "Did you get into trouble with the ski patrol?" she demanded.

"No," I replied. "They let us go."

"You're lucky," Ashley said. "They could have kicked you out of the resort!" She paused. "This is all Christina's fault," she said. "You've been acting weird ever since she got here."

"Well, what about you?" I shot back. "You've been acting weird ever since you met Noah! How can you be so mean to a nice guy like Buddy?"

"What?" Ashley's face reddened. "I don't know what Buddy told you, but I wasn't mean to him!"

"He went to your room to talk to you and you wouldn't even open the door!" I snapped.

"I had green cream all over my face!" she cried. "I didn't mean to be rude to him, but I was running late for my date with Noah—"

"Noah, Noah, Noah!" I shouted. "That's all you care about. Why don't you open your eyes? There's nothing special about Noah. Maybe he's cute, but he's totally self-centered."

"What about you?" she shot back. "When are you going to see Christina for who she really is?"

"You have no idea who Christina is!" I countered.

"You've barely spent five minutes with her. I know she can be a little wild. But she's going through a really hard time right now. She needs a friend."

"A friend wouldn't try to get you into trouble all the time!" Ashley insisted.

"Don't tell me who I can and can't be friends with," I warned.

"Don't tell me which guys I should like!" she said. "I didn't mean to hurt Buddy's feelings. But Noah is the guy for me."

I stared at her. She stared back.

Finally, Ashley bolted for the door. "I need a hot chocolate," she fumed.

"Me, too." I followed her. "I'm going to the lodge."

"No—*I'm* going to the lodge!" Ashley said, speeding up.

"You can't stop me," I told her, walking past her.

We raced downstairs to the lodge. We speedwalked through the lobby. I pulled ahead of Ashley and pushed open the door to the lounge.

I stopped dead in my tracks. I couldn't believe what I was seeing.

Ashley stopped behind me. She stared into the room and gasped.

Two people were snuggled together on a love seat in front of the fire. It was Noah and Christina—and they were kissing!

chapter fourteen

I couldn't believe my eyes. Why was Noah kissing Christina? At first I thought it was some horrible mistake.

Mary-Kate grabbed my hand. I'd just had dinner with Noah that night! He'd kissed my hand—and he'd kissed me good night. How could he be kissing Christina now? It seemed impossible!

I kept staring, trying to change what I was seeing, to make them stop. But they didn't notice me and Mary-Kate. They just kept kissing.

Finally I couldn't take it anymore. I turned around and ran.

"Ashley—wait!" Mary-Kate chased after me. I ran all the way back to my room and flung myself on my bed. Mary-Kate sat beside me and rubbed my back.

I waited for the tears to come. But they didn't.

"I'm sorry, Ashley," Mary-Kate whispered. "You were right about Christina—and I was wrong."

I sat up and hugged her. "But you were right about Noah," I admitted.

"We were both wrong—and both right!" Mary-Kate said. I laughed. "Are you okay?" she asked me.

I nodded. "It hurt, seeing Noah kiss someone else. But then I remembered something. At dinner tonight he kind of bored me. I guess I don't really like him as much as I thought I did."

Mary-Kate smiled. "I'm so glad! And I'm sorry we fought. I know you were just looking out for me."

"And you were looking out for me," Ashley added. "That's what sisters are for."

Later that night I lay in my bed in the dark, waiting for Christina to come back. At last the door to our room cracked open. Christina tiptoed in.

I sat up and flicked on the light. "Oh!" she cried, startled. "I thought you were asleep."

"So, I'm just wondering . . . how could you do that?" I said in a low, even voice.

"Do what?" she asked.

"You knew that Ashley had a crush on Noah. She even had a date with him tonight!" I said.

Christina tried to look innocent. "What are you talking about?"

"Don't lie to me," I warned her. "We saw you two in the lounge."

"So what?" Christina said. "It's a free country. And it's not like he's Ashley's boyfriend."

"But what about Ashley's feelings?" I asked. "She was really upset!"

"You know what? I don't have to take this from you," Christina huffed. "You don't get it, do you, Mary-Kate? The rules don't apply to me. I do what I want, when I want. If someone gets hurt that's their problem."

"I can't believe how selfish you are," I cried. "I can't believe I was ever friends with you."

Christina grabbed her suitcase and started stuffing her things into it. Then she zipped the bag and snatched it up.

"I'll find somewhere else to sleep tonight," she said. "And I'm catching the next flight back to L.A." She left the room, slamming the door behind her.

I lay back on my bed and sighed. *Good riddance,* I thought. *Some friend she was. What was I thinking?*

epilogue

"**M**ind if I hitch a ride with you?"

A slim guy skied up to Taylor as she waited in the lift line. It was almost her turn to get on, and she was by herself. She checked the guy out. He looked about twenty and wore a cool red racing outfit. Even with his hat and goggles on she could tell he was cute.

"I don't mind at all," she told him. They inched forward as the lift line moved. When they reached the front of the line, the lift came, and they rode up the mountain. It was a beautiful day.

"Been in Utah long?" the guy asked.

"Four days," Taylor replied. "And you?"

"A few weeks," he answered.

"Lucky you," Taylor said.

He kicked his skis back and forth. "Yeah. But it didn't turn out the way I planned."

Taylor laughed, thinking of all the disasters she and her friends had been through on their trip. "Our *plans hit a snag or two, or five," she said. "But you know, in the end the trip turned out to be a blast."*

"Same for me," the guy said. "It's the experience that's important."

"I'm Taylor," she said.

The guy shook her gloved hand. "Alexander."

They rode in silence for a few minutes. Taylor admired the snow-covered pine trees along the mountain ridge, etched against the bright blue sky.

"You know what I call this?" Alexander waved his hand toward the landscape. "Heaven on a hill."

Taylor smiled. "Heaven on a hill. I like that."

The lift reached the top of the mountain and they skied off. "Want to ski together?" Alexander asked.

"You sure?" Taylor shot back. "Because I took a lesson and learned some new moves, so watch out."

"Hmmm," he said playfully. "Practically an Olympian. Well, I'll try to keep up with you."

They took off down the mountain. Taylor felt great, but Alexander was unbelievable. Taylor could tell the guy was a serious skier.

They shussed to a stop at the foot of the mountain. Kylie, Jenn, and Charly had stopped for lunch and were just taking off their skis.

"Hey, Taylor." Kylie waved them over. "Up for lunch?"

"Your friend is welcome," Jenn added, nodding at Alexander.

"Thank you," Alexander said. "But I've got to train."

"Train?" Taylor cried. "You're the best skier I've ever seen."

Alexander laughed. "Not quite. Maybe I'll see you again, Taylor."

"I hope so," Taylor said.

"Have a good lunch," he said and skied off toward the lift.

"That guy is cute," Jenn said.

"How can you tell?" Taylor said. "We never saw his face!"

"That was one amazing vacation," Kylie said. "And I'm so glad we got our baby back!" She pressed the accelerator and the Mustang convertible zoomed down the highway.

In the seat next to her, Taylor whooped happily and shook her hair in the breeze. It felt great to be back on the road in their Sweet Sixteen birthday car!

"You got your baby back, baby back, baby back," Toast sang from the backseat.

"Joshua, you are so adorable," Jenn said. Kylie glanced at them in her rearview mirror. Jenn and Toast kissed. Charly, sitting on Toast's other side, made a face.

Toast looked great, Kylie thought—all cleaned up and handsome. He and Jenn made a good couple.

"What do you mean you got your car back?" Charly asked. "Where did it go?"

"A car thief saw it one day at a diner," Kylie explained. "He fell in love with it and decided to take it for a test drive."

"A twenty-seven-day test drive," Taylor added. "Can't blame him, I suppose." She tapped her sister on the shoulder. "Hey, Kylie—it's my turn to drive."

"You will," Kylie promised.

Taylor sighed. "That sounds so familiar."

"Are you excited about school, Charly?" Kylie asked. Charly's dad had agreed to let her go to school in L.A.

"I am excited," she said. "But nervous."

"You have us." Taylor pointed to herself and Kylie.

"And us." Toast squeezed Jenn's shoulder.

A newspaper on the floor of the backseat flapped in the wind. Toast reached down and pulled it up. "Do you want this paper?" he asked. "It's getting ready to blow away." He glanced at the sports section. "Look, Taylor—here's an article about Alex Reisher, that skier you're in love with."

"I'm not in love with him," Taylor insisted.

"There's a picture of Reisher on the slopes," Toast went on.

"Hey." Jenn tapped on the paper. "I recognize that outfit. Do you know who's in this picture—skiing *right next to superstar Alex Reisher?"*

"Who?" Taylor asked.

Jenn passed the paper to Taylor. Taylor studied the picture, then let out a gasp.

"That's me!" she cried. "The mystery guy I skied with the other day was Alex Reisher!"

She bounced up and down in her seat. Kylie grinned.

Taylor clutched the paper to her chest. "That was the best trip ever." She sighed.

"The best," Kylie agreed as she drove off into the sunset.

THE END

Ashley stopped the VCR and pressed Rewind.

"That was great!" Lauren cheered as the movie ended. She and Brittany clapped and whistled.

"Two thumbs-up!" Brittany agreed.

"I'm glad you guys liked it," Ashley said. "We had a blast working on it."

"Well," I reminded her, "there were a few bumps along the way."

"True," she said. "But they were totally worth it. We found a happy ending, right?"

"Right," I agreed.

Ashley glanced at the clock. "Oh, no!" she cried. "I'd better hurry up and change. My date will be here any minute!"

Brittany raised an eyebrow. "Date? Who's your date?"

Ashley laughed. "You'll see when he gets here." She dashed upstairs.

Brittany and Lauren turned to me. "Who is it?" Lauren demanded. "Tell us!"

I grinned. "I think I'll let it be Ashley's surprise."

"So whatever happened to Christina?" Brittany asked. "Have you seen her since you got back?"

I shook my head. "She's living with her mother now. Jake couldn't believe it when I told him about her. He had no idea she'd gotten so wild."

The doorbell rang. I jumped up and ran to the door.

"That must be Ashley's date!" Lauren said. "I can't wait to see who it is!" She and Brittany followed me.

I opened the door.

"Hey, Mary-Kate. Is Ashley ready?"

Buddy smiled at me. He was dressed in his white Elvis Presley costume, his hair greased into a pompadour.

"Almost," I said. "Come on in, Buddy." I ushered him inside. "Lauren and Brittany—this is Buddy."

"Buddy!" Lauren cried. "I don't believe it!"

Buddy looked confused. "Have I met you before?" he asked Lauren.

"They just watched *Getting There*," I explained.

"I told them all the behind-the-scenes dirt."

"Yeah." Brittany grinned at him. "We've heard all about you."

"Don't worry," Lauren added. "It was all good."

"Is that Buddy?" Ashley called from upstairs.

"Yeah," I answered. "Are you ready to go?"

"I'm ready," she replied. "The question is—are *you* ready for me?"

Ashley appeared at the top of the stairs and paused. Brittany and Lauren burst out laughing at the sight of her.

Ashley, too, was wearing her Elvis costume. She ran downstairs and kissed Buddy hello.

"You look excellent," Buddy told her.

"Mega-excellent!" Lauren added. "But why are you guys both dressed like Elvis?"

"We're going to an Elvis party," Ashley explained. "Night of a thousand Elvises."

"It's going to be hilarious," Buddy put in. "But we'd better get going or we'll be late."

Lauren, Brittany, and I watched as Buddy walked Ashley to his car. He opened the car door for her. Then he got in and drove off.

"He seems like a great guy," Brittany said.

"He is," I agreed. "Ashley really likes him. Everything worked out perfectly in the end."

"Just like in the movie!" Lauren said.

"Yeah." I nodded. "Only better."

MARY-KATE AND ASHLEY SWEET 16™
Win a Cell Phone Sweepstakes

OFFICIAL RULES

1. No purchase necessary.

2. To enter complete the official entry form or hand print your name, address, age, and phone number along with the words "MARY-KATE AND ASHLEY SWEET 16 Cell Phone Sweepstakes" on a 3" x 5" card and mail to: MARY-KATE AND ASHLEY SWEET 16 Cell Phone Sweepstakes, c/o HarperEntertainment, Attn: Children's Marketing Department, 10 East 53rd Street, New York, NY 10022. Entries must be received no later than September 30, 2002. Enter as often as you wish, but each entry must be mailed separately. One entry per envelope. Partially completed, illegible, or mechanically reproduced entries will not be accepted. Sponsors are not responsible for lost, late, mutilated, illegible, stolen, postage due, incomplete, or misdirected entries. All entries become the property of Dualstar Entertainment Group, LLC, ("Dualstar") and will not be returned.

3. Sweepstakes open to all legal residents of the United States (excluding Colorado and Rhode Island), who are between the ages of five and fifteen on September 30, 2002, excluding employees and immediate family members of HarperCollins Publishers, Inc., ("HarperCollins"), Parachute Properties and Parachute Press, Inc., (individually and collectively "Parachute"), Dualstar, their respective subsidiaries and affiliates, officers, directors, shareholders, employees, agents, attorneys and other representatives, and the parent companies, affiliates, subsidiaries, advertising, promotion and fulfillment agencies of the above, and the persons with whom each of the above are domiciled. Offer void where prohibited or restricted by law.

4. Odds of winning depend on the total number of entries received. Approximately 75,000 sweepstakes announcements published. All prizes will be awarded. Winners will be randomly drawn on or about October 15, 2002, by HarperCollins, whose decisions are final. Potential winner will be notified by mail and will be required to sign and return an affidavit of eligibility and release of liability within 14 days of notification. Prizes won by minors will be awarded to parent or legal guardian who must sign and return all required legal documents. By acceptance of the prize, winner consents to the use of his or her name, photograph, likeness, and personal information by HarperCollins, Parachute, Dualstar, and for publicity purposes without further compensation except where prohibited.

5. Ten (10) Grand Prize Winners will win a cellular telephone and 300 minutes of prepaid wireless telephone service. Payment for any additional minutes is at the sole expense of the winner's parents or legal guardian; sponsor has no responsibility for any additional minutes. Approximate retail value: $170.00.

6. Only one prize will be awarded per individual, family, or household. Prizes are non-transferable and cannot be sold or redeemed for cash. No cash substitute is available. Any federal, state, or local taxes are the responsibility of the winner. Sponsor may substitute prize of equal or greater value, if necessary, due to availability.

7. Additional terms: By participating, entrants agree a) to the official rules and decisions of the judges, which will be final in all respects; and to waive any claim to ambiguity of the official rules and b) to release, discharge, and hold harmless HarperCollins, Parachute, Dualstar, and their affiliates, subsidiaries, and advertising and promotion agencies from and against any and all liability or damages associated with acceptance, use, or misuse of any prize received in this sweepstakes.

8. Any dispute arising from this Sweepstakes will be determined according to the laws of the State of New York, without reference to its conflict of law principles, and the entrants consent to the personal jurisdiction of the State and Federal courts located in New York County and agree that such courts have exclusive jurisdiction over all such disputes.

9. To obtain the name of the winners, please send your request and a self-addressed stamped envelope (excluding residents of Vermont and Washington) to MARY-KATE AND ASHLEY SWEET 16 Cell Phone Sweepstakes, c/o HarperEntertainment, Attn: Children's Marketing Department, 10 East 53rd Street, New York, NY 10022 by November 1, 2002. Sweepstakes Sponsor: HarperCollins Publishers, Inc.